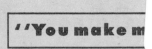 

"Why?" Luke's voice was soft, only for her, his warm breath tickling her ear as they danced.

Natalie forced herself to open her eyes and look up at him. "The way you look at me."

"And what way is that?"

"You know."

"No, I don't. Enlighten me."

Natalie decided, at that moment, that there was no use playing any sort of game with this man. He was a master player, and he would win. She could only hope to survive the ride.

"Like you'd like to take off all my clothes."

He laughed then, and she could sense other people looking at them, wondering what had possessed this man to pay one hundred thousand dollars for the privilege of a single dance.

"You're right," Luke said, totally unrepentant. "I'd like that very much...."

ABOUT THE AUTHOR

A gypsy at heart, Elda Minger has lived throughout the United States and Europe. She currently enjoys life in Palm Springs, California. When she's not writing, she's usually either gardening, dreaming, fooling around or at the movies.

Books by Elda Minger

HARLEQUIN AMERICAN ROMANCE

117—SEIZE THE FIRE
133—BACHELOR MOTHER
162—BILLION-DOLLAR BABY
229—NOTHING IN COMMON
314—WEDDING OF THE YEAR
338—SPIKE IS MISSING
469—BRIDE FOR A NIGHT

Elda Minger

DADDY'S LITTLE DIVIDEND

Harlequin Books

TORONTO • NEW YORK • LONDON
AMSTERDAM • PARIS • SYDNEY • HAMBURG
STOCKHOLM • ATHENS • TOKYO • MILAN
MADRID • WARSAW • BUDAPEST • AUCKLAND

Published June 1993

ISBN 0-373-16489-0

DADDY'S LITTLE DIVIDEND

Chapter One

Darling, you're going to be a daddy....

Natalie Davis stepped back from the dining room table and surveyed her efforts. Everything had to be perfect, for tonight was the night she planned to tell Luke he was going to be a father.

We're going to have a baby....

Her hands shook as she found the book of matches and placed them conveniently close to the white candles in silver candle holders.

In seven months, we're going to be a family....

The linen tablecloth was snowy white, the crystal wineglasses sparkled, the china was one of the patterns she'd picked out, bright jewel-like colors in an Oriental pattern.

Perfect.

She glanced at the clock. Seven thirty-four. Luke had promised to be home by eight tonight. She'd told him this dinner was very special.

He probably thought it had something to do with their four year anniversary, as the date fell within the same week. She was certain he had no idea what she was going to tell him tonight.

And she was doubly certain she had no idea how she was going to tell him.

How different things would have been if they were married, if they were trying to start a family. She probably would have driven straight from the doctor to Luke's office to tell him the good news.

Only she wasn't at all sure he was going to consider her pregnancy good news.

Their relationship was complicated. Too complicated to think about now. Natalie glanced at the clock on the sideboard, knowing it was only a matter of time before things came to a head.

She loved Luke the way she'd never love another. He'd conquered her, body and soul. Luke was an extremely determined man, and what he wanted he usually got. It had only been a matter of time before she'd moved into his Denver penthouse.

She was pretty sure he wouldn't want a baby complicating their lives.

She smoothed the snowy linen with her fingertips, fighting her nerves. Luke would be home very soon, and she wanted to be emotionally ready to tell him.

He worked too hard, but then that was nothing new. Luke Garner was one of the most successful men in the country, and he hadn't gotten that way by coming home early every night. The press had labeled him the Donald Trump of Denver, and he certainly lived up to that title.

Natalie knew several of her girlfriends envied her the relationship she had with Luke. All they saw was that he was tall and darkly handsome, and made a ton of money. They envied the time she and Luke spent at glittering charity balls and other business functions.

What they didn't see was how many nights she spent alone, waiting for Luke to come home.

It wasn't that she didn't have plenty to occupy her time. She was nothing if not an independent woman. But she would have preferred to spend some of that time with Luke.

She was anxious, now, as she checked the clock yet again. Only a few minutes had passed, but it seemed an eternity.

Trying to still her nervous energy, Natalie went into the kitchen and poured herself a glass of freshly squeezed orange juice.

No wine for you. Not any more.

She sipped slowly, willing the minutes to pass more swiftly. There was a part of her, no matter how happy she'd been about the news of her unexpected pregnancy, that dreaded this evening, for she wasn't entirely sure how she was going to tell Luke.

He hadn't exactly made a secret of his feelings toward children. He was a businessman through and through, and liked being able to pick up and go at a moment's notice. That life-style would be finished once their baby was born.

He knew she was on the pill. They'd discussed birth control carefully immediately after they'd become involved. What neither of them had known was that the antibiotics she'd taken for a minor infection had rendered that birth control ineffective, hence her pregnancy.

She'd been shocked when the doctor had told her the news, then filled with a primitive sort of joy she couldn't control. Natalie had wanted to have Luke's child for quite a while, but she'd thought it an impossible dream at best. Almost nothing had been able to diminish her happiness when her doctor had told her the news.

Until she'd thought of Luke. And his probable reaction.

He wasn't going to be pleased.

In her fantasies, she thought of the positive changes a baby would make in their lives. She looked forward to more time with Luke. Time with their child. For the past few months, Natalie had felt they were both running in place but getting nowhere.

It wasn't that Luke didn't love her. He did. He admitted that he'd let her get closer than anyone else. But would that be enough?

At eight o'clock she walked into the dining room, then to the living room. The floor-to-ceiling windows overlooked the twinkling lights of the city and the Rocky Mountains in the distance. The penthouse was exquisitely furnished, but lately Natalie had felt she was living in a cage. A gilded cage, but a cage nonetheless.

At eight-fifteen, she went into the kitchen and checked on the dinner she'd planned. She'd cooked all of Luke's favorite foods in the hope that this dinner might serve as a sort of talisman. Thinking of his reaction to her surprise pregnancy had upset her, made her feel utterly powerless. At least in the kitchen, getting dinner ready, she could operate under the illusion that she had some sort of control.

At eight-thirty, Natalie decided Luke had forgotten about their dinner, or something unexpected at the office had come up and demanded his attention.

By nine o'clock, she knew he'd be home very late from the office, as usual. When she finally noticed the blinking red light on the answering machine, she pushed the playback button reluctantly.

It wasn't as if this hadn't happened before. No one enjoyed Luke's level of success without certain sacrifices. No one worked as hard as he did and still had plenty of free time.

It was just as she'd thought. Mrs. Mitchell, Luke's ever-efficient secretary, with a message that Luke would be working late, and not to expect him back before midnight.

Natalie rewound the tape carefully, but as she performed the small, mechanical gesture, she felt something inside her shatter.

She didn't stop to question the intense emotions flooding her. Though some of the moodiness she'd been feeling had to do with her pregnancy, Natalie knew she and Luke couldn't continue this way. Something had to be done.

By ten, she was packing a suitcase.

Within the hour, she was out the door.

"GOOD NIGHT, MR. GARNER."

Luke nodded in his secretary's direction. He was tired after a long day of negotiations and was looking forward to a good meal, a hot shower and Natalie's soothing, uncomplicated and calming company.

He'd wanted to go home hours ago, but the deal he and his company were putting together with the Akira Corp., a Japanese firm, was a delicate proposition. So delicate that he wanted to handle the details of strategy himself.

Now, as he headed out the door toward the black Porsche parked in the underground parking lot, he thought about home. And Natalie.

There wasn't an evening that he didn't look forward to being with her. They'd been together almost four years, and she still had the power to excite and delight him like no other woman in his life.

He arrived home a little past one in the morning, and quietly unlocked the penthouse doors. When Luke stepped inside, he wondered what Natalie had made them for dinner.

Dinner.

The thought hit him like a freight train. Dinner tonight. Almost a week ago, Natalie had asked him to save this evening for her. She'd seemed nervous and on edge, and clearly it had been important to her.

But not important enough for him to remember.

He mentally berated himself as he called her name. "Natalie?"

No answer.

"Natalie?"

As he came into the dining room, he stopped.

The table, set exquisitely for an intimate dinner for two, made a quietly poignant sight. Physically, it felt like a punch in the gut. To Luke, it simply served as another reminder of how much it must look as if he took her for granted.

He didn't. He thought of her more than any other woman he'd ever been involved with. There were many times during a working day when he had to force himself *not* to think about her.

And that had been a first. Until Natalie, there had never been a woman Luke couldn't completely set aside while in the midst of making yet another one of his deals.

"Natalie? Are you home?"

His voice made the penthouse seem even emptier. She wasn't here, he was sure of that. Natalie might have been mad at him, but she was never one to back down from a fight. She would have made her appearance known, then given him a look, then walked quietly to their bedroom and slammed the door.

He loved her fire. It was part of what had made her a star.

The kitchen was quiet, the dishes done, only one glass in the sink. He checked the refrigerator for a note, then scanned its contents.

She'd put their dinner away. Apparently she'd gotten his secretary's message and decided not to wait up.

Or not wait at all.

He paced through the penthouse, all thoughts of being tired erased from his brain. Tension filled his body as he wondered where she was, what she was thinking and feeling.

When he reached their bedroom, he found the note. Impatiently, he tore the envelope open and read her swiftly written letter.

> Luke,
> I need some time alone. I'm going to the cabin for a few days, to think things through. I'm sure I'll be back before you even miss me.
>   Natalie

He missed her already.

This wasn't like Natalie at all. Normally, she would have remained at the penthouse, waiting for him to come home so she could confront him with her anger. Or she would have been back by now, even if she'd gone out with a girlfriend.

But simply to leave?

He lay on the bed, note in hand, and thought about the last few days.

She'd been acting different, he was certain of that. He'd caught her giving him strange, considering looks. Almost as if she were studying someone from another planet.

Mornings, she was out of bed before he was, and he was an early riser. Usually they found the time for early-morning lovemaking, but that hadn't been the case in the past week or so.

Evenings, she'd been fast asleep when he'd come home, and looked so exhausted he hadn't had the heart to wake her up.

He knew she had a good three weeks before the new ad campaign for Siren Cosmetics had to be shot, so work wasn't the issue. A top model's normal working life was stressful, the pace exhausting, the need for both physical and mental stamina overriding all else. Natalie was rarely sick. She knew how to take care of herself when she was working. One of her cardinal rules, since the early days of her career, was to never let the client down.

Something else is wrong.

Luke got out of bed and walked over to his closet. Once he'd changed his clothes, he threw a large duffel bag on the bed and began packing jeans, shirts, underwear and socks. A pair of boots joined the rest of the clothing on the bed, as did a lap-top computer and several file folders on the Akira Corporation.

Then he called Peter, his personal assistant, and informed him that he was taking a few days away from the office. Luke gave him the telephone number at the cabin, with instructions not to call unless it was an emergency. Peter—wisely—didn't ask him the reason, and Luke saw no reason to volunteer any information. He'd never discussed his relationship with Natalie with anyone, including the press, and he saw absolutely no reason to begin doing so now.

He zipped his bag shut, then swiftly packed the lap top in its case and slipped the various file folders and reports into a sleek leather briefcase.

He wasn't entirely sure how long he'd be at the cabin with Natalie, but he certainly wasn't going to leave her there alone to brood. Knowing women in general and Natalie in particular, Luke decided that letting her mull over her emotions and work herself into a real state was not a very wise tactical move.

It was time to nip this particular problem in the bud.

SHE STOPPED at a Denver supermarket and did some serious stocking up before heading toward the tiny town of Fairplay and the cabin she had built there.

Natalie had no idea how long she was going to hide out in the small Colorado town. She had three weeks until she had to return to work, and she intended to use that time wisely. She had to come up with some answers.

Even though she was used to making obscene amounts of money on modeling assignments, old— thrifty—habits died hard. Fairplay had one small grocery store, the Family Store, and prices were high.

It was smarter to stock up on nonperishable items while still in Denver.

No one had recognized her this late at night, with her hair pulled back beneath a scarf and dark glasses on. She and Luke were one of the star couples of Denver high society, thus she was always cautious and on her guard when she went out in the city.

One of the things she looked forward to and found totally relaxing about Fairplay was that she was simply Natalie to the locals. They didn't know that much about her career. Certainly most of them didn't have an all-consuming interest in high fashion. But more than that, they accepted her, guarded her privacy and let her be.

It was exactly the atmosphere she needed in order to put her jumbled thoughts and emotions in order. She had to make sense out of what she was going to do with her life.

There was no question that she would keep her baby. Though she'd been stunned when her doctor confirmed her pregnancy, and though it had certainly been unplanned, abortion and adoption were out of the question.

Natalie had been caught totally off guard by the flood of emotion that had overtaken her when the doctor had given her the news. She'd been stunned, then fiercely glad. If she was totally honest with herself, she'd admit that she'd wanted to have Luke's child for some time and now that desire was about to become a reality.

But it wasn't fair to force Luke into something he clearly had no desire to do. That was the main reason she'd sought a solution in flight. If she could get away from everyone and everything in her normal life, if she could find some peace in looking at the mountains and the changing foliage on the trees in Fairplay, then she might have a fighting chance as far as figuring out what she was going to do.

HE THOUGHT ABOUT CALLING her. She had a phone in both her car and the cabin, and it wouldn't have been that much trouble to track her down and demand to know what the hell was going on.

But he didn't.

Even though the more he thought about what had happened tonight, the more his temper threatened to get the better of him, Luke didn't call.

She knew what he was going through with this particular deal. If his company managed to pull off a limited partnership with the Akira Corporation, it would be a real coup in the business world.

They understood each other's work, the various pressures and demands—or so he'd thought. He'd never complained when a modeling assignment took her out of the country for days on end, and she'd never complained about the impossible hours he kept when negotiations were in full swing.

Still, he didn't call.

Something—instinct, a hunch, premonition—told him that what he and Natalie needed to talk about had to be said face-to-face.

Fifteen minutes after he finished packing, he was inside his Porsche and on the road toward Fairplay.

SHE REACHED THE CABIN late that night. As none of her groceries had to be refrigerated, she decided to unload them the next morning, after a good night's sleep.

The moon was full, and brilliant moonlight spilled across the front of the log cabin as she walked up the porch steps and slipped her key into the lock.

Once inside, she turned on one of the living room lamps, bathing the large room in a soft glow.

She loved her cabin. Natalie had stumbled upon Fairplay while helping out a friend, but she had made the conscious decision to build herself a retreat during one of the most difficult times in her life. The cabin had stood her in good stead. Sometimes it was enough just knowing it was there. Through all the tumultuous times in her life, her cabin remained a symbol of all that was constant, all that would endure.

It combined an earthy, rustic style with every contemporary comfort one could want.

She hadn't wanted it to be a dark house, so she'd chosen white-stained logs and made sure the design included a soaring ceiling and lots of windows. It was a simple three-bedroom, two-bathroom structure, and it was the closest thing Natalie had ever had to a real home.

But more than that, it was the right place to make important decisions about the rest of her life. And about the child she had created with Luke.

Armed only with a small overnight bag and leaving the rest of her luggage in the car, she climbed the stairs and walked down the short hallway to the master bedroom.

"SHE'S BACK," Otis Crawford said conversationally to his wife when he saw the lights go on across the street. He was sitting in his wicker rocking chair by the bedroom window that overlooked the front of his Victorian-style house.

"Who's back?" his wife, Mae, mumbled, still half asleep. Then she rolled over in bed and sat up, clutching the hand-crocheted afghan in front of her and eyeing him with annoyance for waking her. "What are you doing out of bed?"

"Couldn't sleep," Otis replied. "Now, I wonder what's going on would make a girl drive all the way from Denver in the middle of the night?"

"Get to bed, you nosy old fool."

Otis ignored his wife with the ease of any long-married person. Instead, he rolled a cigarette, looking out the window the entire time.

"You're not smoking one of those foul-smelling things in here, are you?"

"Nope. I'm going to sit on the porch a spell."

"You'll catch your death, Otis."

"I'll bundle up."

Once outside, Otis sat on the porch swing and lit his cigarette. He watched the lights across the way linger in the upstairs master bedroom for a short time, then click off. Sighing, he took another draw on his cigarette.

He liked Natalie Davis, and there were damn few people in the world he could say that about. She was like the daughter he and Mae had never been able to have. When she'd first come to Fairplay, no one had really known who she was, because Fairplay wasn't exactly a fashion-magazine sort of town.

He'd met her one morning while she'd been building her cabin, then helped her finish it. They'd talked a lot while they worked, and during that particular summer he'd come to like and respect her.

To Mae's amusement, he began buying some of the fashion magazines she appeared in. Then, once he invited her over to dinner a few times, Mae had come to like her, as well.

She was a sensitive little thing, which made what she did, in Otis's estimation, all the more remarkable. It was a tough world out there, which was why he preferred his little corner of heaven right here. Nestled in the mountains, close to the clouds and stars, he'd found his own sort of peace in Fairplay.

His dog, Tanner, a black and tan Doberman and Lab mix, butted his head beneath Otis's hand, asking for a scratch.

"Well, puppy dog," Otis said, eyeing the dark cabin silhouetted against the night sky while he scratched the dog's ears, "whatever problems she has will certainly wait till tomorrow."

LUKE WAS TOO KEYED UP to think straight. He stared at the ribbon of highway in front of him and concentrated on his driving.

This wasn't like Natalie. Usually, when something came up, a conflict between them, she was the first one to want to deal with it, to confront it head-on. He'd taught her a lot of negotiating skills, and had been impressed with the way she'd put them to good use during their various arguments.

They didn't fight all the time. If he was honest with himself, the relationship he had with Natalie was the best he'd ever had.

He'd wanted her from the first moment he'd seen her, first for her incredible, elegant, erotic beauty. Her particular brand of beauty would have been enough, but he'd been delighted to find that she had a very clever mind. She challenged him like no other woman he'd known before or since. She kept him on his toes, and he liked that.

He'd wanted her from the moment he'd seen her picture in one of his sister's fashion magazines. The magazine had been open to an ad, and Natalie had gazed out from the photograph, wrapped only in a piece of scarlet silk. He'd taken one look at the photo and felt as if he was struggling for breath. Then he'd picked it up and studied it. The damn photograph had started to turn him on, and he found himself unable to stop staring.

And wanting.

She'd looked like a wild animal, erotic, exciting and totally unpredictable. Her coloring was dramatic, dark brown hair and eyes against startlingly fair skin. But it had been something in her eyes that had captivated him, a challenge posed.

Her body had been everything he'd ever fantasized about, and he'd found himself wondering if she was married.

It hadn't even mattered to him, he'd wanted her that badly. And he was ruthless about getting what he wanted.

He'd called a friend that evening, a client who had connections in the fashion industry. Within twenty-four hours, he knew who Natalie Davis was, what agency she was working for, what level of success she'd attained and that she wasn't involved with anyone.

He set about to remedy that.

He'd found out she was attending a charity ball, and though he loathed the woman who was giving this particular party, he managed to wangle himself an invitation.

Luke smiled ruefully to himself as he remembered. He'd thought it would be a simple matter, impressing a model and getting her into his bed. Getting her out of his system, then moving on, as was his fashion.

Instead, he'd found himself desperate to possess her. He wanted her, he wanted her to belong to him, he didn't ever want to let her go.

And he'd fallen in love. Deeply. Madly. The forever kind of love that he'd believed existed only in novels and films. He'd certainly never had any reason, or evidence, to believe it existed.

And now she was running from him, again.

He took another sip of the black coffee he'd bought along the way. With the heater on high and the strong, hot liquid warming his insides and giving him that kick of caffeine, the chill night air outside didn't have a chance. The dark Porsche smoothly ate up the miles between him and Natalie.

With any luck, he'd be in Fairplay within half an hour.

And he was determined to find out just what the hell was going on.

NATALIE COULDN'T SLEEP.

As soothing as the cabin was, as high-strung and nervous as she'd been the entire evening, as exhausted as her pregnancy was leaving her, she simply couldn't fall asleep. So she lay in the large bed, warm and cozy beneath the blankets and quilts, and watched the shadows flitting along the ceiling.

And thought of Luke.

And remembered . . .

Chapter Two

Four years ago

"Who is that man?" Natalie asked.

"Oh, no, darling, not for you."

She smiled at her date for the evening. Mick Lewis was both an extremely gifted photographer and a good friend. He'd talked her into attending this charity ball as a way of advancing her career.

"Why not?" She couldn't keep her eyes off the stranger. Dark and dangerous, so very handsome in his tuxedo, he was eyeing her with an extremely intense, masculine expression on his face that made her think he was imagining what she looked like without the sexy, sequined slip dress on.

"Luke Garner? My baby, he'd eat you up in a single bite."

"I'm not a child, Mick."

"No," he agreed, running long, agile fingers through his shoulder-length blond hair in exasperation. The bold style suited his leonine features. "But you're my friend, so I'm going to do what any good friend would do and advise you to steer clear of him.''

"Why?"

"Because he'll hurt you.''

They mingled with the crowd, talking and laughing with people they knew from New York's fashion world, but all the while Natalie could feel the stranger's gaze on her. Several times she looked up and caught him staring. He didn't seem remotely embarrassed or ashamed to have been caught in the act. Not sure of what to do, she smiled shyly then glanced away.

But her body betrayed her, realizing a deeper truth she was too nervous to put into words. Natalie could feel her heartbeat pick up speed, could feel the excitement that hummed through her nerves at the thought of getting closer to him.

The elegant, sit-down dinner wasn't bad, and Mick whispered enough truly funny jokes to make the long speeches afterward endurable. After dessert, the society matron in charge of the evening's entertainment stood up and announced that there had been a change of plans.

"In order to raise funds for this worthiest of causes,'' she said, her husky voice booming out over the crowd, "I have decided on an impromptu charity auction. I'm going to ask several of the loveliest ladies here tonight to consent to being part of it.''

Mick glanced at Natalie and rolled his eyes as she stifled an urge to laugh at the expression on his lean face. "Bloody hell," Mick whispered, "Dina Whitney's gone off the deep end again."

"But if it raises money—"

"And what do we get for our money, Dina?" a man shouted out of the crowd, and people began to laugh good-naturedly.

"Why, only a dance, of course." Dina smiled, and Natalie could see she had been absolutely stunning in her prime. She wasn't all that bad now. Natalie watched as Dina, the consummate showman, arched an amused brow and said softly into the microphone, "Whatever else you manage to get is up to you."

The crowd roared, and Natalie turned to find Mick scowling at a middle-aged woman who was approaching their table.

"Don't volunteer," he whispered.

"Oh, Mick—"

"Say you're too shy."

But when the woman asked Natalie if she would mind participating in the auction, she agreed.

"Now you've gone and done it!"

"Oh, Mick, it's for a good cause. What could possibly happen?"

"With Luke Garner looking at you like a wolf after a choice little lamb? You tell me."

"I'll be all right, Dad," she whispered to him. The affectionate endearment was a running joke between the two of them, what with Mick's being almost eighteen years her senior and overprotective, as well.

She was escorted backstage and given a number, then wrote her name on the master list. Number three. Not bad. At least her placement was good. She'd be able to see what was in store for her, but she wouldn't have to wait backstage for a long time.

The first volunteer, Dina's giggly blond seventeen-year-old granddaughter, was auctioned off to her fiancé for two hundred and fifty dollars.

The second, an auburn-haired model Natalie knew from the agency, went for five hundred, after two men got into a bidding war. She walked off the stage gracefully, totally at ease in the spotlight, as if she was on a runway in Paris.

When her name was called, Natalie walked out onto the stage. The lights were blinding, and she couldn't make out Mick's face in the crowd.

"Ladies and gentlemen," Dina called out. "Let the bidding begin."

"Five hundred dollars," said a deep, baritone voice.

"Six," said a voice Natalie recognized. *Mick!* What was he doing?

In the space of a heartbeat she had her answer—and also knew who the other voice belonged to.

"Seven," it said softly, with just a hint of annoyance.

This, thought Natalie, *is a man used to getting his own way.* Despite the warmth of the room, she shivered.

"Eight."

Dear Mick, don't do this.

"Nine." Again, that deep, dark voice.

"One thousand dollars." Mick again.

There was a silence, then Dina was playfully calling out, "Going, going—"

"One hundred thousand dollars."

The last bid silenced the room. Natalie felt her heartbeat speeding up even faster, pounding furiously, sickeningly. Dina Whitney's mouth hung open. She looked like an astonished goldfish. And Natalie didn't even want to consider what Mick was thinking.

It's just a dance....

But it was more than that, and she knew it. No one paid one hundred thousand dollars for a single dance. Luke Garner's bid had been a statement of intent, as surely as if he'd gotten her phone number from the agency, called and asked her out to dinner with him.

She didn't even know him, but she was already afraid of him. The man was power personified. And what did he want from her, to the tune of one hundred thousand dollars?

Natalie glanced at Dina helplessly, trying to hold on to what little composure she had left. The older woman was eyeing her consideringly, her composure firmly in place. Before Natalie had time to think, Dina smiled a particularly pleased smile and banged down the auctioneer's gavel sharply.

"Sold!"

As soon as the other women were auctioned off, the orchestra began to play. Lights were lowered, and the ballroom was transformed into a fairy-tale forest of twinkling white lights twined through the make-believe foliage on the edges of the dance floor.

And Luke Garner came to claim her.

It was a slow dance, and one she was sure she'd remember for the rest of her life.

His glance had unnerved her earlier in the evening, and now his touch affected her even more strongly. She flinched when he put his arms around her just as surely as if his fingers had burned her.

"Are you scared of me?" he asked softly.

That voice. Deep, dark and husky, as if he'd just awakened and was still tangled in rumpled bed sheets. She was scared of what he could probably talk her into doing. Or feeling. Over dinner, Mick had whispered that he was considered a lethal opponent in business.

In the battle of the sexes, this man had a criminal advantage.

"No," she lied, not wanting to give him any of that advantage. She was already in over her head, and she knew it.

She felt his fingers on her chin, raising it gently so she had to meet his eyes.

"Don't be," he whispered. "I'm not going to hurt you."

She didn't answer. Couldn't. The words were caught in her throat, just as she was caught in the most powerful sexual chemistry she'd ever experienced. Natalie didn't know what to do, what to say. Any other relationship she'd had paled to insignificance in this man's powerful shadow.

He was holding her in a way that let her know he'd held a lot of women. And knew how to hold them. She didn't like thinking about his being with anyone else. She could barely deal with the here and now.

"You," he said, his dark gray eyes warm and admiring, "are exquisite."

She couldn't meet his gaze. Natalie closed her eyes, hating the revealing color she felt staining her cheeks. She wished suddenly that she'd worn a dress that covered more of her body, so his fingers couldn't touch her bare skin. And as quickly as she thought it, she knew she could have been dressed in the most Victorian of dresses, and she still would have felt it, would have *known*...

An attraction like this came along once in a lifetime, if a woman was lucky. And if she was brave, she surrendered to it, let herself be led by a strong man into the most powerful, sensual experience she'd ever known.

Yet she was scared. So many emotions rioted through her. Excitement. Terror. Relief that she'd finally found a man who, whether he knew it or not, stormed her carefully constructed defenses and cut straight to the dark, sensual heart of the matter.

He wanted her. She knew that. And she knew why.

Natalie had no illusions about her looks. She'd had too many people discuss her various attributes in front of her for too many years. She knew her face, her hair, her body, with an intimacy most women would never possess. And she was nothing if not objective.

Mick had ruthlessly critiqued her makeup tonight. He'd suggested the red sequined slip of a dress for her body and the French twist for her hair. Faux jewels adorned her ears, and the heels she wore were the highest she had in her closet.

Suddenly deciding she couldn't play the sophisticate, she said the first thing that came into her head.

"You—you make me nervous," she whispered.

"Why?" His voice was soft, only for her, his warm breath tickling her ear as they danced.

She forced herself to open her eyes and look up at him. Even at her height, with her highest heels, she still had to look up at him.

"The way you look at me."

"And what way is that?"

"You know."

"No, I don't. Enlighten me."

She decided, at that moment, that there was no use playing any sort of game with this man. He was a master player, and he would win. She could only hope to survive the ride.

"Like you'd like to take off all my clothes."

He laughed then, and she could sense other people looking at them, wondering what had possessed this man to pay one hundred thousand dollars for the privilege of a single dance.

"You're right," he said, totally unrepentant. "I'd like that very much."

She stiffened in his arms, the blush running up her chest and into her face again. What a fool she must seem to him, with all he had to have done in his life. They were as mismatched as a nun and the devil.

He stopped dancing, and she knew he was studying her intently.

She couldn't look at him.

"How old are you?" he asked. She could hear genuine curiosity in the question.

"Twenty-three."

"How long have you been in New York?"

"Five years."

"And you still blush like that? Incredible."

How could she explain to this man that, six months after she came to the city, Mick had seen her sitting at an outdoor café and introduced himself? He'd asked her to pose for some pictures, and she'd refused. He'd persisted, and convinced her she had what it took to go straight to the top.

Then her modeling career had taken precedence, with its relentlessly early mornings and strict bedtimes. With its endless traveling. She hadn't felt comfortable having any casual affairs of the heart, so she'd lived as cloistered a life as a novice in a convent.

There was only one thing she was certain of at this moment, and that was that she wasn't going to let this man make her feel like a fool.

"How old are you?" she countered.

"Thirty-six."

"And you don't think it's excessive, paying one hundred thousand dollars for a dance?"

"Depends on the dance."

She felt her cheeks warm again, but pressed on.

"Can you afford it?"

The corner of his mouth kicked up in a slight smile. Natalie found, to her surprise, that she liked it. She liked his eyes, as well. They were a cool gray, surrounded with dark, spiky lashes. Attentive, compelling eyes.

She knew he was interested in her. Very interested. But once he found out what she was really about, he'd want to move on to a more sophisticated partner, she was sure of that.

"It's tax deductible. And for a very good cause."

He started moving to the music again, and she found herself following his lead. The first song segued into a second, and Natalie didn't even consider breaking away from him. They continued to move together, their bodies barely touching.

"What's your name?" he asked.

"Natalie."

"Just Natalie?"

"Natalie Davis."

"Natalie. It's pretty. It suits you."

"Thank you."

His lips were very close to her ear, practically brushing the sensitive area.

"Are you seeing anyone?" he asked.

Natalie hesitated. She felt such ambivalence. On the one hand, she was terribly attracted to this man and wanted to tell him the truth and see what happened. On the other, she was frightened of where a relationship with him might lead. One thing she was sure of—she was completely out of his league.

Her heart swiftly overruled her head.

"No."

"I'd like your phone number. Will you give it to me?"

She hesitated for such a long time that she felt like a teenager in the throes of a first crush. Instinct told her this wasn't a man who was going to take her number as a matter of course. He was pursuing her, and she knew he would be relentless in that pursuit.

"I—don't think we'd make such a good match," she whispered, her throat aching. For the first time in her life, she wished she was just a little more worldly-wise.

"I don't agree."

She swallowed, trying to keep her voice from trembling as she asked the next question. But she had to know.

"Are you...seeing anyone?"

"Not anymore."

His answer thrilled her. Her head and her heart began to battle, her head insisting his answer was simply a line, her heart wanting to believe he really meant it.

In the end, she erred on the side of caution.

"Maybe—could you give me your phone number? Then I could call you."

"Would that make you feel safer?"

She nodded her head.

He smiled, and gave her his number.

"You have twenty-four-hour access. It's a private number. Whether I'm in a meeting or out of the country, I'll make sure I get your call."

He was totally overwhelming, and she wasn't sure she was ready for him to invade her ordered life, but even at that moment, she knew she would call him. It might take a little time, but he'd be waiting. He was a predator, and the most successful predators were patient and ruthless. They got what they wanted.

And in this case, if she was totally honest with herself, it was what she wanted, as well.

They danced several more dances, shared a glass of champagne, then he delivered her to Mick and wished both of them a pleasant evening.

She watched him as he strode out of the ballroom.

Mick was in the midst of a conversation that could prove helpful to his career, so she bade him a fast farewell and hailed a cab.

Curled up in the backseat of the taxi with her evening wrap tucked around her, Natalie thought of Luke all the way home. *If just dancing with him exhausted me, what would spending an entire day with him be like? Or a night?*

She didn't sleep a wink. She lay on her side in bed, staring at the small slip of paper on her nightstand that gave her twenty-four-hour access to one of the most powerful businessmen in the city.

Would that make you feel safer? he'd asked while giving her his phone number.

She'd never feel safe again.

But she'd never felt more alive.

HE WAS NOT A PATIENT MAN.

Three days after the charity ball, she arrived at a shoot to find an enormous bouquet of brilliantly colored tiger lilies by the makeup table.

His handwriting on the small card was striking and bold. *Call me. L.*

She stared at the exotic flowers while her makeup was applied and her hair styled. And she wondered the entire time when she was going to call Luke Garner.

It had never been a question of *if.*

She didn't dare tell Mick. He'd been in a temper the day before while photographing her, telling her all about Luke's reputation with women, how many beautiful models and actresses he'd dated and dumped.

Still, no matter what Mick told her, no matter what she read in the tabloids, a part of her heart believed it would be different this time. Her relationship with Luke, no matter how tentative, couldn't be like all the others in his past.

Two days after the flowers were delivered, she called him.

"Luke?" She'd wanted so badly to present herself as a woman of the world, but she could hear her voice. It sounded thin and strained.

"Natalie." That voice. Dark velvet. Soothing and arousing at the same time. It affected her so strongly she couldn't think of anything to say.

But Luke took care of that minor detail.

"I'd like to see you."

Trust a businessman to get straight to the point.

"Yes." It was all she could manage out of her tight throat. Why did her heart have to pound so rapidly? She was sure he could hear it over the line.

"What do you like to do?"

How could a simple, perfectly logical question sound like an invitation to sin? Natalie swallowed, forced herself to breathe again and made her mouth form words.

"I love movies. Or we could go out to dinner—"

"Or we could do both. When are you free?"

She'd had the presence of mind to place her date book by the phone, and now she scanned its pages. "All day Saturday, but not the evening—"

"What are you doing that night?"

He didn't sound nosy, or even demanding. Just curious.

"I'm having dinner at Monique's house." Monique Devereux owned the agency Natalie worked for, and an invitation to dinner at her home was more along the lines of a summons. No smart model ever refused.

"Then why don't I pick you up and we'll go get breakfast, then see what's at the movies?"

This was a man who didn't waste a second. She thought of him coming to her apartment, knowing where she lived, and the thought was overwhelming.

"I'll meet you at a café," she said suddenly, before she considered how it might sound.

He was silent for such a long time, she tentatively said his name, wondering if he was still on the line.

"Why are you frightened?" he asked.

"I'm not scared of you." She had to make him believe that. "I'm scared of me."

She could feel him considering this new piece of information. This time, the silence on the phone was a more comfortable one.

"Fair enough. Name the place."

She gave him the name and address of a favorite café in Greenwich Village, and once they'd agreed on a time, she hung up the phone and stared out one of the large windows in her living room at the brick building across the street.

She felt as if she'd put something into motion, and there was no stopping it now.

SHE ARRIVED AT THE CAFÉ early. He was right on time. Somehow, Luke managed to look a little less threatening in the light of day, wearing well-worn jeans and a bluish-gray sweater.

Natalie could tell he liked her choice of café. It was small, undiscovered as of yet, totally untrendy, run by an Italian family. Every item of food was fresh and prepared daily. She'd found it on one of her walks around the city, and it had become her favorite.

The café was tucked inside an older building in Greenwich Village, and the smells of espresso, peeled oranges and freshly baked bread assaulted the senses. Luke ordered a double espresso, she ordered a café latte, and they settled back to study the movie ads in the *Times*.

"What kind of movie would you like to see?" he asked.

"Something funny."

"So you like comedy?"

"I—I want to laugh. It's been a long week."

Something in the tone of her voice must have caught his attention. "What happened?"

She knew, at that exact moment, that this was a man who would be completely loyal to the few he trusted. She'd done a little reading up on his carefully revealed public persona, and knew that Luke Garner was considered a good friend to some but a formidable enemy to others.

She hoped she never had a chance to experience the latter.

"I don't know. Sometimes I don't think I'm really cut out for this business."

"Modeling?"

"Yes."

"Why?" His eyes were fixed on her as if she was the only person in the world. And Natalie knew how other women had been seduced by this man. This was part of his predatory charm, this unrelenting attention.

Well, he was a businessman, and a brilliant one. If anyone could help her sort out the confusion her thoughts were in, he could.

"I love the work, but I guess maybe I don't have the stamina."

"The killer instinct."

Her eyes widened as she studied him. That was it. Exactly. She'd never thought of it in those terms, but she realized that Luke had, once again, cut straight to the heart of the matter.

"I don't."

"You don't need it. You've got me."

Coming from any other man, the statement would have seemed the height of arrogance. Coming from Luke, said quietly and with total confidence, it was simply a statement of fact.

"I have you," she said uncertainly, not quite knowing what he was getting at.

"I'm a good friend. To the people I like."

"And we're—friends."

"For now, yes."

"You mean, it's conditional?" she asked. That concept made her wary.

"No, I mean I'd like something a little more intimate between us."

"Oh." This man had a very clear idea of what it was he wanted, and had no hesitation about asking for it.

"That makes you nervous." He leaned across the table, his elbows on the edge. "Don't be. This can be whatever you want it to be. Just friends, that's fine. I'll be disappointed, but I've never been one to force a woman into anything she's not completely comfortable with. So you set the pace, Natalie."

"Just friends, for now. Okay?"

"Okay." He leaned back, visually assessing her. "You want to know what I see?"

She nodded.

"I see a woman who has everything it takes to go straight to the top, except for the one thing that would make things a whole lot easier. Self-confidence."

Nothing in his tone or manner made her think he was tearing her down or belittling her. And he was so dead-on it was frightening.

Slowly, she nodded.

"I can't tell you how many beautiful women I see in the course of a weekend. There's a lot of competition out there for what you want, but you've got one thing the rest of them don't have."

"What?" Hearing herself dissected by a master was overwhelmingly compelling.

"You're genuine. I saw it in the photo, I saw it at the dance."

"The photo?"

"I saw you in a magazine my sister had open on her coffee table. Wrapped in red, just like a Christmas present. So I tracked you down."

"Then the dance—it wasn't just a chance thing—"

"There's not a whole lot I like to leave to chance."

"So you knew who I was."

"Partly, yes."

"You knew I was going to that dance?"

"I did."

Comprehension dawned in a sizzling flash.

"You suggested the auction!"

"Dina loved it. And I got to dance with you. And here we are."

She leaned back in her chair.

"Don't back away from me, Natalie. Don't be afraid of me."

"What if I hadn't been at the dance?"

"I would have thought of something." He smiled, and she felt as if she'd been hit in the stomach. Devastating. The man was devastating. "I would have had my company hire you for a shoot under some pretense or other. I would have been on the set. Or I would have wangled an invitation to Monique's dinner tonight."

"Doesn't it bother you, to wield power like that?"

"I've never intentionally hurt someone—unless they deserved it."

A formidable enemy, indeed. In her heart of hearts, Natalie resolved she would never, ever double-cross this man. It wouldn't be worth it.

"So," Luke said, his eyes never leaving hers, "let's order some food and keep talking."

He was like a steamroller, but it was a sensation she was getting used to—and liking.

"Okay."

They continued talking as their breakfasts arrived.

"I'm going to tell you something, and I don't want you to forget it. Every time you're around those other women and you think you don't have what it takes, I want you to remember it."

She nodded, her mouth full of frittata. He was so terribly opinionated, but she loved to hear him. Most of the people she knew didn't express themselves as forcefully as Luke did. He was a refreshing change.

"There are only two things a star needs, and you've got them both. Likability and bedability." He grinned. "There's another word that's usually used. I'm sure you know the one I mean."

She smiled. No one had virgin ears after their first few shoots.

"You've got both qualities. I saw you wrapped in that red silk, and I didn't give a damn what you were selling. I would have bought it. You had me right by the . . . you had my attention. Natalie, you've got it."

"You think so?"

"I know so. What almost every other model has to have redone, from boob jobs to nose jobs, from cheek and chin implants to liposuction, you've got it naturally. But the question is, do you really want it?"

"I don't know."

"You're scared."

She nodded.

"Everyone is. And no one knows anything. You think anyone knows what the flavor of the month is going to be a few months from now? They're all hoping and praying that their guess, their choice, is going to make them some money. And that's where you come in. You look at the camera with those eyes, and you can sell anything."

She took a deep breath. "I want you to help me. And I'll be—a good friend."

"I'll help you. But let me ask you this. Am I wasting my time imagining there could be something more than a friendship between us?"

She blushed then, and the words that came out of her mouth surprised her. "Oh, you *know* you're not! How can you say that, unless you didn't feel even a little bit of what I was feeling that night?"

He threw back his head and laughed, his eyes sparkling, and she realized she'd given him exactly the answer he'd wanted.

THEY DIDN'T LEAVE the café until late afternoon, then they saw two comedies back to back. Natalie was delighted to find out that Luke had a fantastic sense of humor, intelligent, subtle and off-the-wall. He delivered her right to Monique's Upper East Side apartment, and she enjoyed the quiet dinner with the head of her modeling agency.

Monique was very French, and dinner was a quiet affair, the food superb. She didn't directly come out and ask any career questions, she simply made sure she was caught up with her client's life. Blond with cool blue eyes and high cheekbones, Monique had once been a top model. She knew that time at the top was short, and she'd invested the money she'd made and put it into her own agency.

Now, she would never have to work another day in her life.

But she wanted to. The women in her stable were like her family. Appalled at the way women were treated in the business, Monique had vowed things would be different when she was at the helm.

She had been married, once, to a businessman from Germany. They hadn't had any children. He'd died several years ago, and now all her energies were focused on her business.

"So, everything is going well for you?" Monique asked. "No problems?"

Natalie was still flying high from her day with Luke. "None."

"You look happy. Is there a man?"

"A . . . friend."

"A good friend, this man?"

"The best."

Later that night, once she got home, the phone rang. She knew before she answered that it was Luke. She'd given him her number that afternoon in the café.

"How did it go?"

"Fine."

"How about another career step?"

"What?" It was fun, talking to Luke. Each thing he did seemed like a piece of a puzzle, a turn at a game.

"A party. About an hour and a half out of the city. Nothing too formal, just a barbecue."

"There are barbecues and there are barbecues—"

"Henry's a friend of mine. He just happens to be a millionaire."

"Henry who?" she asked cautiously.

He laughed. "Henry Winston."

"Oh, my God." Henry Winston was richer than Croesus.

"Are you up for it?"

She couldn't resist the challenge in his voice. "Of course."

"I'll pick you up at ten." He lowered his voice. "Get a good night's sleep and try not to think about me."

"In your dreams."

HENRY WINSTON'S HOUSE was the size of a French château, and located right on the ocean. The huge stone balcony offered a breathtaking view, and Natalie was glad she had Luke's arm to hold on to as they met the large group of people.

Rock stars and actors, financial wizards and recluses, ex-president's wives, bestselling authors, painters—it seemed as if anyone who was truly anyone in the world was spending Sunday afternoon at Henry's house.

Henry's *estate*, she amended silently.

Luke moved among these people as if he'd been with them all his life, putting them at ease, offering compliments, telling jokes. Yet nothing about him seemed insincere.

When Henry came over to welcome them to his party, she was surprised to see Monique Devereux on his arm.

"Luke! Good to see you!"

Henry Winston was a portly man, with snowy white hair and an open face.

Natalie didn't miss Monique's quick assessment of her hand on Luke's arm. She had a feeling the woman had quickly sized up who her new "friend" was.

"And who is your friend?" Henry asked Luke as he turned toward Natalie.

"The next big star on the modeling horizon," he answered calmly.

"Did you hear that, Monique?" Henry said, his expression amused. "You'd better keep your eyes on this one."

"I already do. She's with my agency."

Natalie couldn't read Monique. It was as if the woman had put up an invisible wall, shutting her out.

"We must find Victor," Henry mused. "Excuse me just a moment."

The three of them were left standing together awkwardly, and even though Luke used considerable charm with Monique, Natalie could tell the woman was not swayed toward liking their particular relationship.

Within minutes, Henry returned, a tall, muscular man with curly blond hair in tow.

"Victor, you must tell me what you think."

"The next star, eh, Luke?" The man's French accent was slight, but there was a distinctly Gallic manner in his gestures. He studied Natalie for almost a full minute.

"She photographs well?" he asked no one in particular.

"Like a dream," Luke answered softly.

"I do need another brunette," Victor said, talking softly to himself. "Is she available next month?"

"For you," Monique said, with genuine affection in her eyes, "I'll make sure she is."

"Then all is settled." Victor grasped Luke's shoulders affectionately, then gave him a swift kiss on the cheek. "Ah, my friend, you do my work for me!"

"Just treat her well."

Victor's green eyes danced with merriment. "I understand."

He and Henry strolled away, and Natalie looked first at Luke, then Monique. "What?"

"That man," Monique said slowly, "will be one of the photographers at what will be the biggest fashion show of the year in Paris. He's helping Maurice Kouris look for new models." She eyed Natalie, her expression fond. "And he's just found another one."

"Paris?" She glanced at Luke. He gently disengaged her grip on his arm, then squeezed her hand.

"I'll leave you two to talk for a while." Then he disappeared into the crowd.

"That's your new friend?" Monique asked. There was absolutely no emotional coloring to the question, and Natalie couldn't tell if she was disturbed or pleased.

"Yes."

"Well, he's done you a favor by introducing you to Victor. I would have waited another season, but it wasn't left up to me."

"Monique, I—"

"No. Don't say anything. You'll be leaving for Paris next month."

Chapter Three

Luke reached the cabin in Fairplay with only moonlight to guide him.

He always felt as though he was stepping back in time when he visited Fairplay. It was a quaint little town, the houses a curious hodgepodge of gingerbread cottages, log cabins, Victorians and small, nondescript frame houses.

The population hovered somewhere around five hundred people, give or take a few. A lot of the townspeople still used wood-burning stoves for heating their houses, as well as propane. Many of the bathrooms boasted claw-footed tubs.

The town basically consisted of a hardware store, a general grocery store, a post office, a laundromat, the courthouse, a few curio and souvenir shops and a few restaurants. The old hospital had closed down. There were several bars and two hotels, the Hand and the Fairplay. And, of course, Mae's Golden Nugget Café.

But there still wasn't a single stoplight in town.

Some things never changed.

There also weren't any streetlights on Clark Street, where Natalie's cabin was located. All the houses were dark as Luke drove down the deserted street. Most of the townspeople went to sleep early and awakened with the sunrise.

The locals were friendly and welcomed visitors. A familiar saying around Fairplay was, "We have ten months of winter and two months of company." And it was true. You could witness a snowstorm any time from September to June.

It was a simpler kind of life, a more natural way of living. He knew that simplicity had been part of the powerful pull on Natalie, and had been one of the prime reasons she'd chosen to build a cabin in this small Colorado town.

He parked the Porsche on the dirt road in front of the cabin, not wanting to block her Explorer in the driveway. Uncurling himself from the front seat, he stretched the kinks out of his lower back, then walked slowly up the drive toward the front porch.

He stopped halfway up the drive. It was a beautiful cabin. The light logs seemed almost silver in the bright moonlight, silhouetted against the stars. He hadn't fully appreciated it when Natalie had built it. If he was completely truthful, there had been moments when he'd been nothing but angry with her.

He'd felt that she'd upset herself with needless worries and anxieties. She saw all the shades of gray in a decision. He was much more black and white. Uncomplicated. They were both very emotional, intense people, and in the course of their relationship had needed time apart.

For a while, that time apart had come naturally. She'd been in Europe on a shoot, he'd been in Denver. She'd been in New York, he'd been checking out properties in Seattle. Almost six months had gone by when they'd barely seen each other, and both of them had been miserable.

But when she'd gone to Fairplay to build the cabin, he'd been angry with her. Angry because he'd thought she'd simply given up. He'd thought she was hiding, running away to Fairplay so she didn't have to deal with harsh reality. And throwing away both a beauty and a talent that few women had in equal shares.

Luke hadn't realized how therapeutic building a cabin from the ground up would prove to be. For both of them.

He knew she considered the cabin her sanctuary. And he knew she considered it more of a home than either the penthouse in Denver or the co-op in New York. Luke put that particular piece of information in the back of his mind, where he could mull it over and try to come up with some sort of answer.

For now, all he could do was let her know how sorry he was for missing the dinner. And make sure she knew he was here for her, whatever she needed.

But missing pieces of this particular puzzle still bothered him. It wasn't like Natalie to run away over a missed dinner, no matter what the celebration. There was something else going on here, more to this than met the eye.

It was so quiet he was conscious of it. The wind blew gently, rustling tree branches, giving the cold evening just that little extra chill. It would be good to go inside where it was warm.

He reached the porch and walked across it as quietly as possible.

Luke had already decided he wasn't going to wake Natalie up. If she woke of her own accord and came downstairs, that was one thing. But it would do no good to start a discussion that might possibly escalate into an argument, when they were both so tired. Whatever it was could wait for the morning.

She'd seemed exhausted lately, and looked emotionally vulnerable. He hadn't had the heart to wake her the last few mornings, even though there wasn't a day he didn't wake up wanting her.

He'd thought she might be trying to conserve her energy for the cosmetics shoot. It was going to be a rigorous assignment, as she had signed an extremely lucrative contract to be the exclusive spokesperson for the entire Siren line.

He left his duffel bag, briefcase and laptop case in the Porsche and let himself in as silently as possible. Luke entered the living room and sat down on the couch. He hadn't been to the cabin in a while, and noticed immediately a few things had changed.

Despite it being a residence that wasn't used every day of the year, it had a warm, lived-in look. She'd whitewashed all the floors, lightening the wood but still allowing the grain to show through.

He had to admit, she'd had incredible vision in creating this place. He'd imagined a log cabin as being a rather musty, dark dwelling, lacking any of the comforts of home. Natalie, in creating this light, airy cabin that was usually flooded with natural sunlight, had proved him wrong.

The furnishings were simple and sturdy. The oversize windows, double-paned, were bare of any curtains or blinds. The sofa he sat on was deep and comfortable, a rich hunter green. Natalie loved deep, jewel colors, and she'd accented the rest of the living space with brilliant blue and warm brown touches. Every color came from nature.

The lamp on the oak end table was fashioned of weathered copper, and he knew how it would gleam if the light was turned on.

He didn't want to flood the room with soft light. Luke sat in the dark room, enjoying the play of moonlight over familiar objects.

The massive fieldstone fireplace that rose to the top of the vaulted ceiling had a split-log mantel. It had always been Natalie's favorite place for framed photographs, old and beloved toys and all the little possessions she'd attached memories to.

There weren't that many family photographs. He wasn't close to his own, except for his sister, and Natalie had grown up in a series of foster homes.

Luke smiled, remembering. Once their relationship had begun, she'd managed to get several pictures of the two of them together. These were always on display in whatever residence they were occupying. And several small, framed photos always traveled with her, packed carefully in her suitcase.

Now, most of them rested on the mantel. When he looked at that photographic history, it gave him a sense of peace. No one had ever bothered to chronicle any of his personal life in pictures.

No one but Natalie.

He eased his boots off, then piled a few of the large throw pillows on one end of the long, comfortable sofa. A soft wool afghan was draped over the back of it, and he knew from past experience that it was big enough to cover him and keep him warm for the rest of the night. Natalie had designed a comfortable home, and he appreciated it now that he was taking the time to really see it.

Luke peeled off his socks and put them by his boots. His shirt soon joined the small pile of clothing and, clad only in his well-worn jeans, he wrapped himself in the afghan and eased himself down full-length on the sofa.

Within minutes, he was asleep.

THE MORNING SUNLIGHT streaming in through the windows woke him up. For a moment he was disoriented, not knowing where he was. Then he recognized his surroundings and relaxed.

Barefoot and still shirtless, he climbed the stairs slowly, not wanting to make any noise.

He entered the master bedroom silently. And stopped in the doorway, surveying all that was inside.

She was lying in bed, curled up beneath a mound of covers. A bright patchwork quilt was on top of the rest of the blankets, and seemed the one spot of vivid color in the room. The bed was one they had picked out together, with a carved wooden headboard. A hurricane lamp was on the nightstand by the bed, and the rest of the room was simplicity itself.

The master bedroom had been designed with comfort in mind, complete with high ceiling, stone fireplace and balcony. But the focal point of the room had always been the large bed, and Luke found his gaze straying back to Natalie.

The room was bathed in soft, early morning sunlight. The sky, already an incredible shade of blue, could be seen through the large windows. As in the living room, Natalie hadn't wanted any curtains in this room, either. She'd come here, she'd told him once, to be close to nature, not barricade herself away from it.

Luke walked over to the bed, careful not to make the slightest sound, and looked down at her. She was wearing a white nightgown, old-fashioned, with lace at the throat and wrists.

Her thick, dark hair was unbound and spread out over the pillow as she slept. She looked, Luke thought, like a fairy-tale princess come to life. Like Snow White or Rose Red. Sleeping Beauty.

She still looked tired. He noticed the delicate smudges of color beneath her eyes, the tension around her mouth that even sleep couldn't erase. And he wondered what it was that troubled her so deeply, and if she would share her problem with him.

Gently, Luke lowered himself onto the bed. All the while, he watched her, hoping she wouldn't wake up. He positioned himself so that he was lying outside the tangle of blankets and quilts. Slowly, he eased his arms around her and moved closer so they were lying next to each other.

She stirred for just a moment, a frown creasing her forehead, and he held his breath. It was clear she needed a little more sleep. He felt it when she settled down among the blankets again and relaxed.

He watched her for a while as she slept, then fell asleep again, feeling more content than he had in a long time.

WHEN NATALIE WOKE, Luke was lying in bed next to her.

She couldn't move, because his arm was pinning down her long hair. Not that she wanted to. What she wanted to do was watch him sleep a little bit, and hope that her morning sickness wouldn't be too vile.

Eventually she'd have to get up. But for now, she was simply glad Luke was here.

In a way, she felt guilty. Halfway to the cabin, she'd remembered he was in negotiations with a Japanese company and that this deal meant a lot to him. She hadn't expected him to come after her, but now, seeing him lying next to her on the bed, she was glad he had.

He needed a shave. There was dark stubble on his face. He looked tired. There were dark circles beneath his eyes.

Yet he looked wonderful.

She was wondering how she was going to extricate herself from his grip and sneak downstairs to try to sip a cup of ginger tea when his eyes opened. She watched as he struggled out of sleep, as his gaze slowly focused on her.

And she wondered how she was ever going to explain.

"HI," HE SAID SOFTLY, wondering how she was going to react.

"Hi." She reached for his hand, brought it to her lips and kissed it.

"Hey." He touched her hair, smoothing it away from her face. "Natalie, I'm sorry I forgot about dinner."

"It's okay."

Something was wrong. He could feel it, sense it. Her expression was guarded, and her dark eyes seemed . . . sad.

He wondered if he'd barged in where he wasn't wanted. If there was one thing Luke understood, it was an individual's desire for privacy.

"Did you not want any company?" he asked, hoping she wouldn't ask him to leave.

"No. I'm glad you came up. This is nice, just the two of us. Nowhere to go, nothing to do. Time for each other."

He tried to remember the last vacation they'd taken together, and couldn't. Luke resolved that they would have a few days together, no matter what.

"I forgot about the deal," she said.

"Which one?"

"With that Japanese firm."

"Don't worry about it." The deal meant nothing to him when he was worried about her health. Why hadn't he noticed how tired she'd been earlier?

"Why don't you sleep a little longer? I can make us breakfast later."

The thought of any kind of food made her want to gag. Pregnancy heralded many physical changes, and her hormones were going wild.

"Maybe I will sleep a little bit more. But I need to get up for a minute, first."

He waited for her to make a move, then saw the laughter in her eyes.

"You're lying on my hair."

"Oh." What was it about this woman that she could make him as self-conscious as a teenage boy? He'd conquered the business world by the time he was in his early thirties, and she could reduce him to emotional mush with a look. At least he had the composure to remain calm.

He sat up in bed and watched as she walked across the room to the bathroom.

She stayed in for a long enough time that he began to get concerned.

"Nat?" He knocked softly on the bathroom door. "Are you all right?" And he realized, as he knocked, that she'd never locked the bathroom door before.

"I think my stomach's a little upset."

"Let me in."

She looked like an angel that had fallen out of the sky, pale and miserable. And embarrassed. He wondered why. It was impossible, over the course of almost four years together, not to have seen some of the worst sides of each other. They'd helped each other through sickness before. Why did this feel so different?

"Can I get you anything?"

"Some tea. Ginger tea. It's in the kitchen."

He'd grown used to her treating herself with home remedies. He'd been concerned enough to read up on them to make sure they were safe. Natalie felt everything through her stomach, and when she was upset, it reflected that upset literally.

"I'll be right back."

He brewed a cup of tea, then brought it to her in bed. She was under the covers by then, propped up on a pile of pillows.

He watched her as she took a few sips of the tea. Her color was bad. She really looked awful. He wondered if she was sick and didn't want to worry him.

But now wasn't the time to ask.

"I would have made you some toast, but there wasn't any bread."

"I've got groceries out in the car."

"I'll unload them."

When he opened the Explorer and saw the amount of food she'd brought with her, he knew that when she left she'd been planning to stay in Fairplay for some time. She'd bought eleven bags of groceries. Luke knew that, no matter how much money Natalie had made as a model, she wasn't a woman who bought food carelessly.

What exactly was going on?

It's as if she's already left me. The thought slipped into his mind as he put the groceries away in the large pantry. *As if she's already decided not to come back.*

Luke knew he was a calm, rational man. But the thought of losing Natalie was more than he could handle. He wouldn't ask her any questions until she was feeling better, but then he was going to demand some answers.

He fixed her two slices of toast, then took the stairs two at a time and returned to the master bedroom.

She was sitting up in bed, looking marginally better. She took the plate from him, managed to eat one slice, then set the rest down on the nightstand and lie back down.

Then she held out an arm for him indicating he should join her. He lay down in bed, this time easing beneath the covers and taking her into his arms. Anything remotely sexual was the furthest thing from his mind. Luke just wanted to hold her.

"Mmm."

He could feel her breath, warm on his neck, and he kissed the top of her head.

"It's perfect," she whispered.

"What is?"

"This. Right now. Lying in bed with you and feeling safe and secure. It's a perfect moment, and I wish I could hold on to it forever."

"We've got forever, baby."

She sighed then, and he felt the emotion trembling through her entire body. He could feel her shutting him out, putting up defenses.

"Nat, will you answer one question?"

She nodded.

"Are you really sick?"

"It's just an upset stomach."

"No, I don't just mean what happened this morning. Are you ill?"

She seemed to sense the fear within the question, for she drew back until she could meet his gaze. Her eyes were filled with tears.

"No."

"Then what's wrong?"

"I think I'm just tired. And scared."

He could feel himself relaxing. This he understood. Natalie always managed to work herself into a state whenever she embarked on something new, and the job as Siren's spokesperson was going to be a demanding one.

He drew her against his chest, then stroked her hair, his touch light and soothing. He felt her relax against him, heard her breathing become deeper and slower, felt her heartbeat slow down.

"I'm with you, baby. Nothing bad is going to happen. I won't let it."

He felt her lips move against his neck and guessed she was smiling.

"I've always envied your confidence."

"Ah, most of it's a front. Half the battle's convincing other people you're confident." He continued to stroke her hair, holding her, hoping to soothe her to sleep.

"Luke?"

"Hmm?"

"Would you give me something?"

"Anything."

"Would you stay with me for the next week and not ask any questions? Could we just be together and enjoy each other?"

"Sure." He didn't hesitate for a heartbeat, certain that he could delegate responsibilities at the office. Whatever anyone else couldn't handle, he could phone or fax in.

His instincts told him he hadn't gotten to the bottom of this mystery yet. But if it was only Natalie's nerves over her new contract, they could both do worse than take a week off from the pressures of their lives and spend it with each other.

And it gave him seven days to figure her out.

"Go to sleep, baby."

"Luke?"

"Shh."

"All the best times of my life have been with you."

He felt her relax against him and start to slip into sleep while he thought about the remark she'd made. His eyes stung. What the hell was going on?

HE FIXED HER BREAKFAST later that morning, but she didn't feel like eating and they argued. He insisted she make an appointment with Doc.

"He'll see you today if you give him a call and tell him it's an emergency."

"But it's not—"

"You're exhausted, you're not eating—come on, Nat! I know you better than that! Humor me and go see Doc."

He knew she was scared of going to the doctor and had an almost phobic fear of hospitals. But he also knew she liked and respected Doc Harte.

The man was in his late sixties, but he'd grown up in Fairplay and had been taking care of her people since graduating from medical school. He'd claimed he'd always known that this small town up in the mountains was where he wanted to practice medicine.

Doc's office was located on Front Street, and there wasn't a man, woman or child in town who didn't adore the old man. Or keep trying to marry him off to one of the available widows.

Luke phoned and made the necessary appointment, then drove her to Doc's office. It was a slow day, and Fairplay's doctor welcomed them both into his office.

Doc Harte had always reminded Luke of a skinny, cynical Santa Claus. Doc was a tough old bird, as most of the older people in Fairplay were. They'd seen too much, over the years, to be soft and sentimental. The mountains brought out either the best or worst in people, and it was certainly not a region for the faint of heart.

Luke waited outside the examining room and idly tried to read a copy of the *Rocky Mountain News*. But his thoughts were inside, with Natalie. He felt ashamed of bullying her into this appointment with Doc, but was relieved at the thought of the older man checking up on her.

If anyone could find out what the trouble was, Doc could.

"I'M PREGNANT," Natalie said softly.

"I see." Doc offered no judgment, simply observed her. "Are you happy about having a child?"

"Yes. But it was my fault."

"And how do you figure that?"

Briefly, she told him.

"That's nobody's fault. Neither of you knew." He made a few notes on the pad in front of him, then said, "So this baby wasn't planned. How does your young man feel about your being pregnant?"

Natalie sighed. Doc's old eyes were shrewd and didn't miss much. "I don't know. I don't think he's going to be happy."

"I'd ask him."

Just like Doc. Straight to the point.

"He—he doesn't want children."

"How do you know this?"

"He said so."

"When?"

She was sitting with Doc in his comfortable office, down the hall beyond the two examining rooms. Unlike most modern doctors, Doc Harte liked to talk to his patients. "Take his time," as he so often said. His firm belief was that often all a person needed was to talk about something, share problems with someone who would really listen.

As Otis joked, Doc had been into stress management before the phrase had been coined.

"Early on. When we were dating."

"What did he say?"

"That he—wasn't a man who wanted a family. Or marriage. That he didn't want to be—encumbered."

"And how long have the two of you been together?" Doc's bright blue eyes were kind as they studied her.

"Almost four years."

"That's as long as some marriages."

"I know that."

"But you're not going to tell him."

"Not . . . yet."

"He's the father of your child. He has the right to know."

"I know. I'll tell him. It's just that I've asked him to stay with me for a week, and I'd like a few more days with him in case . . . because . . . if he doesn't want . . ." She couldn't get the words out, and she put her hand over her eyes as she felt them fill with tears.

"I understand."

He handed her a box of tissues and held her hand until she composed herself.

"Have you got a good doctor back in Denver?"

"Yes. But I'm staying right here. I'd like you to deliver my baby, if that's all right with you."

"I'd consider it a privilege. Are you taking prenatal vitamins?"

She dug them out of her purse and he checked them.

"Morning sickness?"

She nodded.

"A little ginger tea helps. So does peppermint. And keep some crackers by the bed, or get that young man of yours to make you some dry toast."

"Okay."

Doc gave her a reassuring smile. "Natalie, find the right time to tell him. I have faith in Luke, I think he'll make an excellent father."

"But he doesn't want babies."

"Babies are one thing. *Your* baby is another."

They talked a little longer, and Natalie could feel her tension easing. By the time she went out into the waiting room to see Luke, she felt as if she could handle whatever happened to her.

"There's nothing wrong with her a little rest won't take care of," Doc said, striding out into the waiting room behind Natalie. Luke had stood up when she entered the room, and now he focused his attention on the doctor. Natalie held her breath, knowing Doc would keep his promise to her but nervous all the same.

"So there's nothing I should be worried about?" Luke asked.

"Not right now, no. But if she doesn't get the rest she clearly needs—and I know she's a stubborn little cuss—I don't want to think of what might happen."

"I'll see that she gets some rest," Luke said, then held out his hand to Doc. The two men shook hands, and as Luke held the door open for Natalie, she heard Doc's voice.

"Remember what we talked about, Natalie. And if you ever need an ear, I'm here."

SHE TOOK ANOTHER NAP, and managed to make a late lunch for the two of them. They ate their sandwiches in front of the fireplace, then she slept on the sofa while Luke made some business calls.

Mae sent over some fresh bread from the café, and a casserole full of beef stew for dinner. Natalie pushed enough around her plate to convince Luke she'd eaten, then retired early.

He came to bed a little later, and she feigned sleep, wondering how she was going to tell him. The less they talked, the fewer questions he asked, the better. For now.

Doc was right. Luke had the right to know he was going to be a father. In a very selfish way, she was taking the choice right out of his hands. She'd felt so guilty about the slipup with her birth control pills, but Doc had convinced her it wasn't her fault.

She felt Luke roll over in bed, felt him put his arm around her and hold her gently against him. Her eyes stung as tears blinded them. It was a peculiar type of torture, to be lying in bed, so close to him physically and yet so distant emotionally.

Lies and half-truths never brought a couple closer.

Not wanting him to realize she was crying, she tried to think of happier times. Earlier times. Natalie took a long, slow breath, closed her eyes and thought of Paris.

Chapter Four

She'd been to Europe before, on other fashion shoots. But never during the midst of a new season, and never as a model on the runway.

Backstage was chaos, models rushing to have their hair restyled or slip in and out of various outfits and shoes, makeup artists behaving temperamentally, and all the while the designers watching over the entire production to make sure their creations were displayed to the best advantage.

Natalie found most of the women friendly. There were two she especially liked. Jane, an English model, with long, fiery red hair, startlingly blue eyes and a voluptuous figure. And Marta, a Swedish model with silvery blond hair, pale blue eyes and a sweet, innocent smile.

Everyone stayed away from Michelle. Tall, with striking, angular features and short, glossy black curls, the woman had competitive poison running through her veins. She didn't miss a chance to criticize someone just at the crucial moment before she stepped through the slit in the curtain and started onto the runway.

The house was packed, the excitement palpable. Rock stars, movie stars, journalists, wealthy matrons, fashion editors from major magazines—everyone was out front, ready for a show to end all shows.

"He's in the audience. Front row," Jane whispered to Natalie as she wriggled into a long, slim red evening gown. The beading was intricate, the gorgeous material cut on the bias. It was a dress only a woman with an exquisite figure could wear.

Natalie knew Luke had made plans for dinner late in the evening after the show, but she hadn't thought he would want to watch it. Didn't fashion bore men to tears? She didn't have time to get nervous as her long, dark hair was given one last quick flick with a brush.

"Wet your lips, darling!" the stylist whispered, then she was walking purposefully toward the slit in the curtain. One of the backstage helpers parted the heavy material. A model swept in, and several dressers descended on her as Natalie walked onto the brightly lit runway.

She knew the lights would pick up the bright, sparkling beads sewn on the evening dress, but she wasn't prepared for the collective gasp of astonishment that rippled throughout the packed crowd.

She didn't dare look for Luke. She was here to do a job, to hold her body in a precise way that showed this particular creation off to its best advantage. To walk slowly, sinuously, down the runway.

To make every woman in that room believe that if she bought this particular evening gown, she'd look just as good.

Walking slowly, steadily, fluidly, she made it to the end of the runway. Pause. Pivot. Show off the gown. The designer's creations were the true stars of this fashion show. Then she turned, and the audience gasped again, for this particular creation was cut very low, all the way to the small of her back.

She started up the runway toward the curtain and was surprised at the spontaneous outbreak of applause.

I'll bet Luke started it.

As she slipped inside the concealing curtain, she was jostled roughly and would have fallen if one of the stylists hadn't caught her in his arms. Glancing up, she saw Michelle brushing herself off, glaring at her with an obvious expression of distaste.

"Why do we have to put up with incompetence from the new girls, Maurice? She wouldn't even be here if it wasn't for that rich boyfriend of hers!"

"Stuff it, Micki." This was from Jane, her blue eyes snapping. "You should be so lucky, to have even one night with a man like that!"

Michelle glared at the English model, then turned to the army of stylists who were intent on creating yet another look.

Natalie didn't have time to get upset. Between the moment she arrived backstage and the instant when she stepped on the runway again, she was undressed, poked, prodded, styled and recreated for another turn down that brightly lit aisle.

The evening gowns toward the end of the show always drew the biggest response. This year, designers were responding to the public's wish for total fantasy, and they'd topped their previous year's efforts with creations in iridescent satin, beads, sequins and taffeta. The colors were glorious—gold, black, red, electric blue and hot pink.

Natalie turned her head when she felt a large hand on her shoulder.

Maurice Kouris. He was the undisputed star of the season, a Frenchman who liked his women to look like women. He was married to a popular French actress, and the couple spent most of their time in their château outside Paris. He ventured into the city to show off his creations, which pleased lovers of fashion no end.

"Not that one. Put her in the black lace."

Natalie didn't have time to think. She was hustled back in the large room, and the same stylists began to prepare a totally different look, under Maurice's softly spoken commands.

Unlike other designers, he was competent and cool and rarely lost his temper. Natalie had been in awe of him for the first few days they'd rehearsed the show, but now she simply knew him for what he was—a genius with fashion and an extraordinarily kind man.

"Put Marta in the red taffeta," he instructed calmly, indicating the evening gown Natalie had almost slipped into. "We're changing the lineup."

Though the show was rehearsed over and over, a designer had the right, at the last minute, to make changes as he or she saw fit. So much depended on the public's perception, and their response.

Natalie had barely sat down at the makeup table when the argument broke out.

"That's *my* dress!" Michelle hissed. She'd just come off the runway, and one of the stylists had informed her of the change in the lineup. "Maurice, I—"

"Quiet." At six foot six, with his large build and black hair slicked back into a tiny ponytail, Maurice Kouris was an imposing figure. "I've decided I wanted a change."

"But you promised me—"

"Nothing. Can't you hear their response? They like her."

Natalie closed her eyes as the stylist passed a brush through her hair, twisting it into an elegant chignon. If Michelle had disliked her before, this little incident would earn her the woman's total and complete hatred.

"It's because that millionaire she's screwing is leading a damn cheering section! You promised me that dress, and I'm not—"

"Get her out of here." Maurice's command was quiet, his dark eyes glacial. Nothing was going to ruin his show, and certainly not a mere model's temper tantrum.

As Michelle was escorted out of the room, the designer turned to his assistants. "Put Jane in the beaded jade, Marta in the short silver sequined and Caro in the electric blue mini. But I want Natalie last. And all alone."

He must have seen her expression in the mirror, for he knelt down and put a reassuring hand on her shoulder.

"Don't be upset, I know what I'm doing. You're going to walk down the runway all by yourself. At the very end, I want you to turn each way, then fix your gaze on a point in the room and remain very still until you count slowly to thirty. Then walk slowly back up the runway. Do you understand?"

She nodded her head as best she could while having her makeup redone.

The dress Michelle had fought over was the ultimate in black-tie glamour. Short, made of black lace, the neckline was very low and the beading inspired. The hemline ended way above the knees, and another few inches of the flirty skirt was constructed of see-through lace.

It was a daring dress, and Maurice's favorite.

He led her to the curtain, waited until the last model had slipped backstage, then smiled at her and whispered, "No smile. I want a woman of mystery, *n'est-ce pas?*"

It was the longest walk of her life.

She reached the end of the runway. Poised in front of the entire audience, she turned first one way, then the other. Then she began the countdown.

One ... two ... three ...

The crowd began to whisper among themselves. Cameras flashed, the bursts of light almost blinding. Natalie stood perfectly still, willing her limbs not to tremble.

Thirteen ... fourteen ... fifteen ...

The applause started at twenty-one. It built to a roaring crescendo as people came up out of their seats and showed their deep appreciation for Maurice's creations.

She willed herself not to smile as happiness flooded through her body. On the count of thirty, she slowly retraced her steps and slipped into the slit in the curtain.

"Back out, *minou*," Maurice told her, grinning as he turned her deftly with his large hands and parted the red curtain. "This time, be yourself. Walk slowly, easily, and smile."

She did. She couldn't stop smiling. Without intending to do so, Natalie knew she'd taken the French fashion world by storm. Young, beautiful, projecting that all-American energy Parisians adored, and dressed in the gown of the moment, she smiled into the blinding lights as she made the runway her own.

THE BLACK LACE DRESS was delivered to her hotel room within an hour after the show. There was a note with it, and she smiled as she read the now distinctive handwriting.

Natalie,
   I'll pick you up at eight for Maurice's party. Wear the dress. Bring any friends you want to.

L

Jane and Marta were almost beside themselves at the thought of attending one of Maurice's private parties. They both rushed out the door, determined to find something absolutely smashing to wear. Natalie, tired after the show, took a nap until six, then joined her two friends in getting ready for the evening.

She tried to duplicate the stylist's chignon, and carefully recreated as much of the makeup as she remembered. Jane informed her that Michelle had left the hotel and taken a plane back to the States.

Natalie knew there might be trouble when she returned. She and Michelle worked for the same agency, and Natalie couldn't predict how Monique Devereux was going to react to the news that Maurice had given a first-timer his most stunning creation.

She forced the worried thoughts out of her mind, determined to have a good time.

A limousine picked them up promptly at eight, then took them to Luke's hotel. He got into the sleek black car beside her, looking dangerously handsome in formal attire.

He kissed her swiftly, carefully, on the cheek. Like a friend. Then he turned to her friends and complimented them on their gowns.

"Thank you so much," Jane said quietly. "I've never been to one of Maurice's bashes, but I've heard they're fabulous!"

"I hope none of you have eaten," Luke said. "Maurice is passionate about two things, fashion and food. His personal chef is formidable."

"Eaten?" Marta replied. "None of us has eaten a thing for the past week. We've been starving ourselves in order to get into those dresses."

Luke laughed. He put his arm around Natalie's shoulders and brought her more closely to his side. She melted against him, breathing in his scent, enjoying the warmth that seemed to emanate from his tanned skin.

She knew everyone assumed she and Luke were sleeping together. And she wondered what people would think if they knew he hadn't even really kissed her yet. Not as a lover would.

She knew he was a good friend, doing anything in his considerable power to make her happy. But she was beginning to wonder what he would be like as a lover.

Maurice's party proved to be the stuff dreams were made of. Both Jane and Marta took off to mingle, and Natalie watched with admiration as Jane walked right up to a current rock heartthrob and introduced herself. Marta decided to check out the elegant buffet tables first.

Natalie stayed close to Luke's side, wanting to spend some time with him. She knew he didn't have business in Paris at the moment, and the thought that he had flown across the Atlantic to be with her was a daunting one.

His pursuit of her spanned the globe.

Maurice came over with his wife, Aimee, and gave Natalie a bear hug and kiss. "You will be in trouble with Monique, but don't let her yell too much. How unhappy can she be, with all the money she is going to make with you?"

"Thank you," Natalie said, knowing her heart was in her eyes. This talented giant of a man had made her first experience on a Parisian runway a memory she would never forget.

"The only thing is," Maurice teased, settling his arm possessively around his wife, "now I do not know if they liked you or the dress."

"I like her, *and* I like the dress," Luke said, his grin infectious. His gaze lingered on the expanse of leg revealed by the lacy skirt. "Very much."

They joked and laughed for a few moments more, then Luke steered Natalie toward tables piled with French food.

"Luke," Natalie began nervously.

"What?" His eyes were so alive, his expression so open. For a moment she just stared at him, wondering at destiny and how this man should have come to be her friend.

"Did you . . . did you start the applause when I was out on the runway?"

"No. You did that all on your own." He caught her hand and placed it against his chest as he looked down at her upturned face. "Scout's honor."

"You were a boy scout?"

"Never. But it's the truth, Natalie. I didn't do a thing." He kissed her hand. "Now, come on, Cinderella, this is your night to shine. Let's get something to eat and then do a little dancing!"

JANE AND MARTA both decided to stay later than Luke and Natalie, so Luke left the limousine at their disposal and suggested he and Natalie walk for a while.

Normally, Natalie would have been a little afraid, walking through a strange city at night. But with Luke at her side, she felt she could do anything. Even fly.

She laughed at the thought, and he squeezed her shoulders gently.

"What's funny?"

"You."

"Thanks."

"No, it's just . . . isn't there anything you don't think you can do?"

"Not much."

Brash, bold and opinionated. Even with all the money at his disposal, she knew many women would consider Luke to be a difficult man. He wasn't a male who would be tamed easily. He would want to do most things on his own terms.

She knew from the gossip she'd heard about him that he was a man who played to win and that his business competitors generally prepared themselves to lose. Luke possessed incredible energy and a relentless drive to stay at the top.

And he would move heaven and earth for the one he loved.

As they walked along the dark streets in Paris, Natalie wondered what it would be like to be loved by Luke. Or if he would ever come to love her, as opposed to simply wanting her.

She'd brought an evening wrap, but it was no match for the elements. The night was clear, the weather crisp, cool and windy. It smelled like rain. Luke had given her his evening coat, had slipped it around her shoulders before they'd started their walk.

She didn't know where they were going and didn't really care. Rounding a corner, they came across a bistro that was still open. The light inside looked golden against the blue-black night. Muted conversation and the clinking of glasses and cutlery could be heard on the quiet night air. Smells of simple French cooking wafted out, and Natalie sniffed appreciatively.

"Still hungry?"

"I couldn't eat another thing!"

"Did you have a good time?"

"Yes. It still all seems so unreal. Almost like it happened to someone else."

"I know what you mean."

She slipped her arm around his waist, and he pulled her more closely against him. "Thanks for coming to see the show, Luke."

They rounded another corner, and a light drizzle began to fall. This street was full of shops, closed for the night. Streetlights bathed the area with a gentle glow, and Natalie could see the fine, misty rain against the light.

"Cold?" he asked.

She nodded.

He turned her toward him, then swiftly buttoned the coat she was wearing. Then, taking her hand, he led her into one of the darkened doorways.

"We'll get a cab," he said, positioning himself so that he stood between her and the chill, damp street. "But there's no use getting wet in the meantime."

"You must be freezing." She laid a hand on his shoulder, and he turned toward her.

It happened in a heartbeat, perhaps because they were finally alone. Before, they'd been around other people, in cafés, at the movies, at parties. Or they'd talked on the phone, safely apart.

Now, with just the two of them in a dark doorway in the middle of the rain, she looked into his eyes and felt the emotions between them.

And realized the truth.

She couldn't stop looking at his eyes, the way the dampness in the air caused his lashes to spike. He was responding to her, to this energy between them.

She couldn't control the fine tremors that filled her, couldn't stop her lips from trembling when she tried to form words. Any words, anything to delay what she now realized was inevitable.

He stood looking down at her, excitement in his eyes. Controlled excitement. And she realized he was wiser than she in matters of the heart, and that he hadn't lied to her. He was going to let her set the pace.

She met his excitement with her own, and smiled slowly. There were times when she secretly thought of herself as a coward, not taking every physical, mental or emotional challenge she should. Not being up for wild adventures. But looking at this man, she knew that what had to happen between them had to happen now.

"Don't make me ask you, Luke," she whispered, moving her lips so they barely brushed his ear.

"You're sure?" he whispered, and she gripped his forearms tighter to stop the shaking.

She nodded and leaned away from him, her back resting against the wall. She watched, feeling lethargic and almost boneless as he carefully unbuttoned the buttons of the coat. When his hands slid inside and grasped her around her waist, she closed her eyes.

This wasn't about friendship. This was about the most beautiful moments that could occur between a man and a woman.

He lowered his head toward hers, brushed his lips against her cheek. She turned her face, seeking, wanting something she wasn't even sure of. His face was shadowed, but the soft light from the street was fully on her own, and she knew that what she felt for him was clear in her eyes. She wondered what he felt for her, mere seconds before his lips met hers.

Then nothing mattered anymore. Both of them sighed into each other, melted into each other. Simply surrendered.

He stepped closer, toward the warmth of her body and the shelter of the oversize coat. His body felt hot and hard and strong as he pressed her gently against the wall. His lips were warm and firm, and she made a soft little strangled noise, a surprised noise, when he effortlessly parted her lips and explored her mouth with his tongue.

She could feel that tongue throughout her body as the trembling increased. And she knew, with female certainty, that she wasn't going to be able to control this encounter. She wasn't going to be able to stop him.

Because she didn't want to.

Her hands came up, first cupping the sides of his face, then touching his hair, then gripping it tightly. He kissed her cheekbones, her temples, her eyelids, then her lips, this time making her knees almost give way. But he held her, his fingers were digging into her waist, his body was pressed against hers, and she knew he wouldn't let her fall.

The rain was coming down harder as he continued to kiss her. Time seemed to be suspended, and she had no idea how many minutes had elapsed before she felt his hand move smoothly upward and cup the full underside of her breast.

She exhaled into his mouth, breaking the kiss. He looked down at her while he touched her, and she couldn't open her eyes. Not out of any sense of shame, but because the feelings he was drawing out of her body were exquisite.

His fingers gently pulled at one nipple, already distended and hard. Her breath came out in short, staccato little sobs as he aroused her, letting sensation build slowly, inevitably, overwhelmingly.

He stepped closer, and her legs parted as he positioned himself between them. She could feel him now, all of him, including the heavy, full erection that pressed against her. It made her shiver, let her know how much he wanted her, how violently his body was responding to hers.

She didn't make a sound when he stepped back and eased her arms out of the coat sleeves, then coaxed one lacy strap over her arm. The scanty bodice of the dress fell away, revealing one breast, the dark pink nipple fully aroused. One arm supporting her back, the other cupping her bottom, he lowered his head and touched her nipple with his lips.

His mouth seemed hotter, much hotter, as he took in the swollen tip. Natalie clutched the back of his head with one hand, her fingers threaded through his hair. He'd pinned her other hand behind her back so the strap couldn't slip and thwart his conquest of her.

Her eyes closed, she gave herself to him, knowing there was no going back from this moment.

Moving one hand from behind her back, he cupped her other breast. Her flesh seemed heavier, more sensitive, and she felt herself craving his touch. Natalie arched her back so she filled his palm completely. He kissed his way up her chest to her neck, then claimed her lips again.

She felt every touch he made on her highly sensitized skin, yet when he stepped away from her and gazed down at her, she realized he'd effectively slid her straps over her arms and the bodice of the lacy dress to her waist.

Her breasts felt cold for just an instant, exposed to the night air, then he was against her again and all she could feel was the warmth of his shirt front. He'd already unbuttoned his tuxedo jacket, and now he crushed her against him as they kissed.

The street was totally silent except for the sound of rain sheeting down. The doorway was a deep one, and he moved her farther in, blocking anyone's view of their intimacies with his own big body.

He took the pins out of her hair, watching as the long, dark strands settled over her shoulders. He pushed them back as he caressed her breasts, kissed her, whispered how much he had wanted her, how badly he wanted her now....

He kissed her until she was wild for him, until the wet heat between her legs was all she could feel. When his hands inched up her stockings, she bit her lip and rested her head on his broad shoulder. She'd worn elastic-topped, sheer black stockings with this dress, and a G-string. Nothing to spoil the line.

Nothing to stand in his way.

Nothing to prevent a total conquest.

When he touched her, through the tiny scrap of black silk, she moaned, hearing the sound as if it came out of someone else's mouth. His fingers found her most sensitive spot with unerring accuracy, and he began to rub, lightly, gently.

She whimpered, and he found her mouth, kissing her into silence. He continued to touch her, to stroke her, until her legs trembled and her stomach muscles jumped. Then, right on the brink of her release, he stopped and slowly slipped a finger beneath the elastic of the G-String.

"Luke," she whispered, anxiety in her voice. Her body felt as if it wasn't her own, as though it was about to shatter apart.

"Shh." He traced the swollen sensitized female flesh, then slipped his finger inside, ever so slowly, and she felt as if she were burning.

Again he brought her to the brink, then slipped his hand beneath the G-string and slid it down her legs. He helped her to step out of it, then picked up the scrap of silk and put it in one of his pockets.

He pulled the lacy skirt over her hips, then slid his hand between her legs once more, touching, rubbing, pressing against her in complete intimacy.

"Do you like that?" he whispered, his voice low and rough.

"Yes...."

She arched against his relentless fingers, crying out, desperate for the sensual release he finally gave her.

She wasn't sure how long she leaned against him. Slowly, she raised her head from his shoulder. She'd had her cheek pressed against his tuxedo jacket, her hair was tumbled over her eyes. She pushed it back with a shaky hand and looked at him.

His expression was fierce, his manner tense, and she took his face in her hands and kissed his lips softly. She felt terribly intimate with him. Safe. Secure.

She wanted to explore everything with this man.

"Luke," she breathed softly, then let her hands wander down his chest, past his belt, until her fingers settled on the hard masculine ridge. She watched his shadowed face, watched the tension in his facial muscles as she slowly lowered his zipper.

He kissed her then, fiercely, swiftly, and she shuddered with the knowledge that their coupling was going to be fast and hot and primitive. It would be better that way, it would hurt less. It was time to make her virginity a thing of the past, and she wanted Luke to be the man who would make her a woman.

She touched him, tentatively squeezing until he closed his fingers around hers and taught her how he wanted to be stroked. The length and heavy thickness in her hands was intimidating. It seemed impossible that they should fit together.

For a moment she panicked and thought of twisting away and telling him not to continue. Then he touched her hip, caressed her skin with his fingertips, and she caught fire again.

She wouldn't have been able to stop him if she'd tried, he was too impatient for her, and within a minute he had one of her legs around his hip, positioning both of them for his total possession.

She thought she was ready for him, she knew she was as sexually aroused as she'd ever been, and she loved him with all her heart. But nothing had prepared her for the reality of his penetration. She tried to relax, but once he'd positioned himself, his first thrust was strong and sure.

She cried out, the pain negating her desire, and he stopped all motion, then moved slightly away from her, breaking their intimate contact.

She shuddered violently, too ashamed to look at him, feeling so utterly wretched she wished she could simply be swallowed up by the earth.

He touched her, but this time it was different. All traces of sexual feeling were suppressed as he smoothed her skirt over her hips and swiftly adjusted his clothing. Then he took her in his arms and held her.

The warmth from his body seeped into hers, and she held on tightly, feeling as if she'd failed him.

"I'm sorry," she whispered. Her eyes stung, and to her horror, one fat tear slipped past her eyelashes, then another.

"No, baby. No. I rushed you."

He held her until she stopped shaking, then helped her fix the bodice of her dress and slip her arms into the sleeves of his coat. The rain had stopped, and he managed to hail a cab within a few minutes.

"I'll take you back to your hotel," he whispered, holding her against him as the driver glanced at them in his rearview mirror and smiled.

"No—I want to stay with you. We can—" She glanced at the driver, then whispered close to his ear, "we can try again."

He gave the driver her address.

She gave the driver his.

Finally he gave in to her wishes and within the hour they were upstairs in his hotel suite.

"You're freezing," he said as she sneezed. "You need a hot bath and a glass of brandy."

She liked the way he took care of her. He took a hot shower, while she soaked in the separate tub. He dried her off, with nothing sexual in the way he touched her.

The hotel provided them with white terry robes, and once outside the bathroom, he took her to one of the bedrooms. She slipped off the robe and crawled between the sheets, then looked at him expectantly. He was sitting at the foot of the bed in a robe, his wet hair slicked off his face.

"Why didn't you tell me?" he asked.

"I wanted to get it over with. I thought—you'd want a woman with more experience."

He moved across the bed until he was sitting next to her.

"It's nothing to be ashamed of. It should be celebrated."

"I didn't exactly plan it that way. I just made the decision to wait until someone very special came along."

He picked up her hand and kissed her wrist. "I'm flattered."

"We could still—"

"No. I'm going to take you someplace very special, where we'll have more than an evening together, and we can celebrate this new part of our relationship."

She considered this, then nodded. The long night had tired her, and she saw the wisdom in his decision.

"Are we still friends, Luke?"

"More than ever." There was a devilish glint in his eyes as he bent and kissed her forehead, then walked silently out of her room.

She woke up later in the night, restless. He'd left the light on in the living room, so she pulled on her robe, belted it and left the bedroom.

It didn't take her long to find the master bedroom. As her eyes got used to the darkness, she could make out his form beneath the blankets.

Without giving herself a chance to lose her nerve, she let her robe fall to the floor, then slipped beneath the covers.

As soon as she touched him, he woke up.

"Natalie?"

"I was thinking," she said, rushing the words. "I can understand not wanting to actually do it all tonight, but there's no reason I couldn't...couldn't..."

This was more difficult than she'd thought.

"Yes?" he said, his voice husky, rough with sleep. Did she also detect a hint of laughter?

"Do what you did to me. For me."

He pulled her into his arms, and she could sense his smile in the darkness.

"Darling, I took care of that problem hours ago."

"Oh." She started to struggle out of his grip and out of his bed.

He didn't let her.

When she rolled against him, she felt his arousal.

"I thought you—"

"I did."

"Then why—"

"I want you. Again." He levered himself up on his elbows and looked at her flushed face. "But I'm selfish, and I want two weeks of nights with you, even a month if I can manage it. I want to take time with something as special as your innocence."

He kissed her then, and she felt safe and protected in his arms.

"I'm glad you waited for me," he whispered as he broke the kiss.

"I'm glad I found you," she answered. "Or you found me."

"You were well worth the chase. And," he said, with just a hint of a smile in his deep voice as he took her hand in his own and guided it exactly where he wanted it, "as long as you're here, I wouldn't mind your idea at all."

Chapter Five

Luke awakened early, as the Colorado dawn washed the sky and filled the cabin's master bedroom with light. He studied Natalie, still sleeping, and decided she looked a little better. He felt considerably relieved. If Doc said all she needed was a little rest, he'd make sure she got it.

He thought about what they would do once Natalie woke. She could take it easy while he puttered around and saw if there was anything that needed fixing in the cabin. It was funny, the way Natalie was about things like that. Even though she worried more than any single person he knew, and had a whole raft of inner demons waiting to come out and torment her, she was one of the most independent and self-reliant women he'd ever met.

It hadn't always been that way. When he'd first met her, she'd been young and terribly innocent. Qualities that had helped her work but had almost destroyed her professionally. She'd trusted people too much, believed in always looking toward the bright side. He'd learned early on in business that most people possessed a little of both qualities, good and bad.

But one thing he knew with a vengeance—never get between a lion and his kill. Luke had learned never to get between a certain kind of person and what they really wanted. You could get badly, badly hurt.

He'd wanted to protect her from the world, from the disillusionment he'd known she would face sooner or later. Yet he'd had to watch while she made her own mistakes, learned her own lessons. Selfishly, he'd thought of keeping her at home in a fabulous house, locking her away from what he knew was on the outside. But Natalie had been meant to play a part in the world, and there was nothing he could do about that.

She wouldn't have let him, anyway.

He knew she had the desire to be out in the world, highly visible, successful. The various modeling assignments were like challenges to her, and they were fulfilling.

But Natalie was a woman full of paradoxes. Going out to dinner at New York's finest restaurants, taking on assignments that put her in the center of crowds of people. Then building this cabin out in the middle of Colorado.

Yet he could understand the seductive pull of a place like Fairplay. The people were genuine, and very few had ulterior motives. They simply were what they were.

He'd never taken the time to notice how peaceful it was. The evening before, the night sky had filled him

with a sense of wonder. He'd taken a walk and seen
the aspens. Natalie had told him about her favorite
trees. How, in the fall, they seemed to glow at dusk.
He hadn't quite known what she meant, but when he
saw the golden foliage, he'd understood.

He hadn't shared a lot of time at the cabin with her,
and he felt selfish as he admitted the fact to himself.
She'd always been after him to drive to Fairplay more
often, to leave work behind, to take better care of his
health. Ironically, it had taken a health crisis of her
own to get him here. To get him to slow down.

A soft knocking on the downstairs door brought
Luke out of his thoughts. Easing out of the large bed,
he pulled on his jeans and padded downstairs. He
opened the door to find a stocky, barrel-chested man
on the front porch, a black and tan dog by his side.
The man looked vaguely familiar, with his thick head
of steel-gray hair and friendly hazel eyes. He was
dressed simply, in jeans, boots and a red plaid shirt.

A name flashed into his mind, and he gambled on
it.

"Otis?"

"Yep. Nice to see you, Luke."

It shamed him, in a funny way, that this man should
remember his name and he should have to guess at his.
Otis and Mae. Luke's mind lost the last vestiges of
sleep and kicked into high gear. Otis had helped Natalie build the cabin. Mae, his irascible wife, ran the
Golden Nugget Café on Main Street.

"Come in," Luke said, indicating by gesture that his invitation extended to both man and dog.

"C'mon, Tanner," Otis said, then softly snapped his fingers. The large dog whined, then trotted in the door beside his master.

"Coffee?"

"Wouldn't refuse a cup. Mae never makes it strong enough."

Luke smiled at the hint as he walked into the kitchen, man and dog at his heels. Otis and Mae had been good neighbors to Natalie, and it suddenly struck him that she'd probably spent more time up here with the two of them than with him.

He made the coffee, familiar with the workings of the kitchen. Remembering a box of muffins among the groceries, he dug around in the cupboard until he found them, then heated two in the microwave.

"Mae doesn't like those things," Otis remarked. "Has one at the café, but won't have one at home."

"They're useful."

"I think so." Otis sighed, then perked up when he saw the plate with two muffins on it. "Pecans. That's right, she likes pecans. Likes the pecan pie at the café. I'll have Mae send over a slice tonight. Doc tells me she's a little under the weather."

If it had come from anyone else, Luke would have been annoyed. But he knew Otis, and the old man had probably seen the Porsche in front of Doc's office and put it all together. Doc was out and about all over town, and it wouldn't have taken Otis more than a few questions to wangle the truth out of the man.

Luke also knew that Otis adored the ground Natalie walked on, and that went a long way in making Otis all right with him.

Tanner cocked his head and barked, and Otis gave him a mock-fierce look.

"Don't just demand it, Tanner! It's always nicer to ask politely."

"Ask for what?"

"Oh, Natalie keeps his favorite dog biscuits in a tin on that top shelf. He's just being a pest."

But Luke checked the tin, and took out two biscuits for the large dog. Tanner lay down on the kitchen floor and began to crunch them up.

Luke, always a master at negotiation, poured Otis a cup of black coffee and joined him at the small farm table.

"Help me out, Otis."

"With pleasure. What's the problem?"

"She's not taking care of herself. You know Natalie, she's working herself up over a new deal she has with a cosmetics company."

"I know the one. Siren."

It astounded him that Otis had so much information at his fingertips. How did he get it, living out here in this mountain town?

"Read it in the *National Star*. Called Natalie up to congratulate her about it, and we talked."

I'll be damned.

"Knew she was coming up here, too. She called me ahead of time and asked me to come on over and turn on the heat. She gave me a key. Mae and I have it, just in case."

Luke considered the older man across the table from him. It seemed there was a lot he didn't know about the life Natalie had made for herself in Fairplay. He didn't begrudge Otis his role in her life, and now he was sure he could trust the man.

"Doc said she has to rest. I'm prepared to stay here as long as it takes."

"Well." Otis took a sip of his coffee, then eyed Luke consideringly. "I think that between the two of us we can come up with a plan to get her back in shape. One woman can't be more of a problem than a herd o' cattle." He glanced out the kitchen window in the direction of his house. "Then again..."

Otis had been a cowboy, but now he was retired. He walked with a bit of a limp. His left leg had been gored by a bull. But, as he was fond of telling anyone who would listen, "It takes more than a little bull to keep Otis Crawford down!"

He liked adventure and excitement, and Luke remembered that Natalie had told him she believed the old man was bored by retirement. His two cronies, Sam and Pete, engaged him in a weekly poker game, but by and large Otis was heartsick for the old days.

Maybe having him help keep an eye on Natalie would be good for both of them.

"Nice car you've got out there," Otis remarked, starting on the second muffin. "Bet it goes pretty fast."

"It does." Luke smiled. "Want to take it out and try it?"

"Lord, no. But sometime if you're planning on taking it out for a spin, I'd like to come along."

"I'll remember that."

Both men glanced up when Natalie came into the kitchen. She'd slipped a red flannel robe over her nightgown, and her hair fell in dark brown waves over her shoulders. She looked as if she'd just gotten out of bed, and Luke was grateful to Otis for the distraction he provided. If it had been just the two of them, Luke might have wanted to sweep her off her feet and take her back upstairs to bed.

He frowned as he noticed her feet were bare. Whenever she could, Natalie took off her shoes, and today was no exception.

"Otis!" She threw her arms around the old man and gave him a hug, then kissed him on the cheek. Otis flushed pink, then patted her arm.

"I've been having a little talk with your young man."

Natalie flashed a grin at Luke, and he was heartened by the fact that some of her spirit seemed to have returned. "Nothing serious, I hope."

"Man talk. Cars, cattle, wood, that sort of thing. Your woodpile's getting low. Luke and I could get that taken care of before the snow starts."

"That would be a big help."

Luke watched her as she crossed the kitchen and opened the refrigerator. She eyed its contents for a moment, then shut the door.

"Sit down, I'll make you some eggs," Luke offered, getting up from the kitchen table.

"Oh no, I don't—"

"I think it's a flapjack type of day, myself." Otis stood up, then pulled out the ladder-back chair he'd been sitting on. "And I know you like my flapjacks. Whatever fixings you don't have, Mae will. Now sit down, and I'm going to make you a proper breakfast."

Natalie stood, looking at both of them, and Luke could sense her hesitation. But Otis didn't give her a chance to refuse.

"You know the story behind my flapjacks, but I bet your young man here doesn't. Now Luke, I'm going to tell you all about it."

Luke took a sip of coffee, already amused. It was obvious Otis was a practiced storyteller.

"It's the damnedest thing, how it happened that I came to understand flapjacks. I'd never had much desire to learn how to cook anything. But out on the trail, if we'd relied on the stuff Cookie fixed for us, we all would've starved to death...."

OTIS SWEET-TALKED Natalie into an entire breakfast complete with flapjacks, real maple syrup, bacon, orange juice and even biscuits. Luke simply kept the coffeepot going and threw a few more dog biscuits in Tanner's general direction.

Later, after Otis had talked him into joining the weekly poker game and they had thoroughly discussed the best possible way to replenish Natalie's wood supply, the old man and his dog headed toward home.

"He's a sweetheart. I hope you don't mind him," Natalie said as she watched him walk across the street.

"I like him. And you're right. He's bored."

She turned toward him, her delight in the fact that he'd remembered evident on her face. Still dressed in her nightgown and robe, she walked over to his side and put her arms around his waist.

"You know what I'd like to do?"

"What."

"Go upstairs and light a fire in the fireplace. Take a shower. And then," she said, as she touched the side of his face with her fingers, caressing his jawline, "we could fool around a little."

"You read my mind."

THEY TOOK A LONG, hot shower together. They washed each other's backs, he washed her hair, then, wrapped in towels, they proceeded to the bedroom.

Luke lit a fire after he tucked her into bed. By the time he returned to her side, she was already dozing off.

"It must be so boring for you. You come all the way up here and all I do is sleep."

"No, baby, it's fine."

"Maybe we could go to the Golden Nugget for dinner."

"I'm not bored with your company."

"I'd like to thank Mae for the stew. I have to remember to give Otis that casserole—"

"Sleep."

He made several business calls while she slept, then lay back on the bed and thought about his strategy for creating a limited partnership with the Japanese firm.

For the moment, he wasn't worried about Natalie. She'd eaten, she was willing to rest, and with Doc's help, they could get through whatever they were up against.

He turned off the light and was staring into the fire when the phone rang.

Otis.

"I didn't wake her up, did I?"

"She's sound asleep."

"Good. I talked to Mae and asked her if she'd deliver your dinner for the rest of the time you're here. That way, neither of you would have to worry about cooking."

"Otis, I can't—"

"Sure you can. Anyway, Natalie's part owner of the café, so she might as well get a little something extra back on her investment."

That was something he hadn't known about, either.

"Of course. But it's still thoughtful of the two of you."

"Hell, Mae wanted to do it. That summer Natalie built the cabin, Mae lost her sister. Natalie came over every single night and listened to the same stories, over and over. She helped her a lot. I already knew all those stories, so I wasn't good for much."

"She said something about going out tonight. To the café."

"It's getting cold outside. Why don't you come down for lunch tomorrow? Mae's making chili tonight. You know how it's always better the second day."

"We'll be there. And thanks for making breakfast."

"I enjoyed it. She's heard that flapjack story before, and she always laughs at the right parts."

Luke grinned. "Take care of yourself, Otis."

"Same to you."

As he hung up the phone, Luke thought it strange that a man he'd considered little more than a stranger had evolved so swiftly into a friend.

HE WORKED ON the lap-top computer for an hour, then slipped into bed with her. It felt good, these long, lazy hours with nothing to do and no one to see. They hadn't had a long stretch of uninterrupted time in a while, and Luke began to understand the reason Natalie had chosen to build her cabin here.

The fire had died out by the time she woke up. She sat up in bed, and the slight movement was enough to wake him.

"How do you feel?" he asked.

"Better. A lot better."

"See? Doc was right. We'll get you rested up and ready for Siren in no time."

"Hmm." She snuggled against him and pulled the blankets over them both.

"I like this," she whispered.

"So do I," he said, cupping one of her breasts and lowering his mouth to hers. It always felt like the most perfect of homecomings when he made love to Natalie. In bed, she was totally responsive and uncomplicated. It was rare that she'd ever not wanted to make love. Their temperaments meshed perfectly in this area of their relationship.

He didn't want to hurry her, though it had been almost two weeks since they'd last made love. Their schedules, her exhaustion, everything had seemed to conspire to keep them apart.

He was already hard, but when she touched him, he felt himself become even more aroused. Still buried beneath the covers, he kissed her with a mounting urgency. He felt himself racing toward that ultimate union, even though he had not wanted to rush her.

She rolled over on her back, taking him with her, her hands gripping his hips. He settled into the cradle of her thighs so naturally and had to consciously resist the urge to thrust into her.

"Now," she whispered.

He didn't need any more encouragement.

She was ready for him, hot and wet and tight. He pushed inside her, then forced himself to lie still, not wanting to rush toward completion but afraid he might have to.

"Don't," she said. "Don't wait."

He couldn't have if he'd wanted to. As his pleasure intensified, he gave himself over to it and thrust, again and again, racing toward release.

He found it mere minutes later, climaxing powerfully as she held him tightly against her. Almost a minute passed before he could start to roll away.

"Stay with me," she murmured.

It was sensual heaven, lying on top of her, still sheathed in her tight warmth. The master bedroom was growing dark, the fire had died out, and he wondered how long he could remain with her in Fairplay, shutting the rest of the world out while she regained her health.

She kissed him, and he felt himself begin to stir. Softly, slowly, he swelled inside her until he was as hard as he'd been before.

He caught the sides of her face with his hands and looked at her. There was just enough light coming in the large windows so that he could see the look of utter contentment on her face.

He shifted slightly, and watched the changes in her face. Her mouth opened slowly, her eyes squeezed shut, her breathing deepened. Luke continued mov-

ing, determined that this time she should know pleasure to equal what he had experienced.

His thrusting was slow and deliberate, touching her
as deeply as possible. He was attuned to her every
movement, to the way her fingers clenched his back,
then his hips. To the way her breathing began to
quicken, sharpen.

Then it was as if she came alive in his arms, as the
fine tremors of her excitement took her over the edge.
Head back, eyes closed, she cried out and her movements triggered his release all over again.

This time, when he eased himself off her, he kept his
arms tightly around her and pulled her to his side as he
slept.

OTIS CAME BY almost an hour later, with a basket
filled with fried chicken, mashed potatoes, country
gravy, green beans and two generous slices of pecan
pie. He also brought several videos, all comedies.

"I remember reading something about a man who
was ill, and he laughed at some videos and it fixed him
right up. Made sense to Doc, and it makes sense to
me."

"It's appreciated. Did you have dinner, Otis?"

"Ate with Mae. I wouldn't want to disturb you two,
anyway."

"You're never a disturbance. The poker game's the
day after tomorrow, right?"

"At my house. Starts at seven."

"I'll be there."

They ate in front of the bedroom fireplace, and afterward made it through one of the movies and were into the second before Natalie fell asleep. Luke rewound the first tape and washed the dinner dishes, repacking the basket for Otis.

When he went upstairs, he stripped off his clothes and climbed into bed beside Natalie. They'd made it through their second full day in the cabin, and he could already see a decided improvement. If things kept progressing at this rate, within the week Natalie would be back to her old self.

He'd be relieved when she was.

She woke up in the middle of the night from a sound sleep. Wondering what had disturbed her, Natalie glanced around the bedroom, trying not to move too much. Luke was a light sleeper, and she didn't want to disturb him.

He was stretched out across his side of the bed, the covers kicked off. She liked to bundle up in bed, while he didn't like covers on top of him most of the time. She studied him with a new awareness, now that he was the father of the child she carried inside her.

He'd make a good father, she knew that. And she wondered at fate, giving both of them this chance when neither of them had expected it. Things sometimes happened that way in life, and she was a firm believer in listening to what the universe had planned.

Ever since she'd met Luke, she'd felt their relationship was destined. She'd wanted to wait for a very special man. Her father had left her when she was nine, and her mother had been unable to care for her soon after that. The foster homes had never been the stuff of nightmares, but she'd never quite felt at home.

Now she'd found herself a man she could love forever. Or he had found her, she thought, a rueful smile curving her lips. She'd built them a home while he'd gone out into the world and created an empire. And now, a baby...

A family.

A group of people that would make up her home.

She wanted it all so badly she was afraid to hope for it. Luke had said repeatedly that he had no desire for children. But no matter how badly she wanted to have his child, she would never have gotten pregnant without consulting him.

Fate had taken that decision out of her hands.

Doc was right. Luke deserved to know. She'd been so upset about telling him the truth that she'd worried herself sick. Now, she told herself firmly, there would be no turning back. Luke deserved better. As soon as she felt emotionally up to it, and before they left this cabin and headed to Denver, she would tell Luke he was going to be a father.

Her glance fell on the small glass bowl of shells on the nightstand. She'd collected them on the Caribbean island of Aruba, where Luke had taken her. He'd promised her a sensual adventure after their encounter in Paris, and he'd transported her to a world where only the two of them existed.

She moved closer to him, slipping her arms around him and resting her cheek on his chest. He shifted in his sleep, and his arms came around her.

Nestled safely in his embrace, Natalie contemplated her future. If the very worst happened, and Luke ended up walking out of her life, at least she had sensual, magical, emotional memories few other women could match....

Chapter Six

Within days after their night in Paris, Luke took her away to a place where they could have total privacy.

Natalie knew she'd given him her answer that rain-swept night, had told him quite eloquently without any words that she wanted to deepen their relationship. She'd also let Luke know she trusted him above all other men.

She gave over that trust completely, knowing instinctively that he would never hurt her.

None of this stopped her from being nervous.

She worried the entire time she packed her suitcase. What did a person wear on a trip in which she expected to lose her virginity? Knowing Luke, she could have brought absolutely nothing, but she wanted to make things special for him, as well.

She made lists and shopped and tried to plan, but in the end she swiftly packed a suitcase, made all the necessary arrangements to be gone for almost six weeks, then met the sleek, black limousine that pulled up outside her apartment building and slipped inside.

Now there was no turning back.

Luke met her at the airport. He'd had some final business to attend to in order to free up the next few weeks.

Then Natalie was introduced to more of Luke's life.

The private plane took off as soon as the pilot received permission from the airport. Once they were airborne, Luke opened a bottle of sinfully expensive champagne and toasted their flight. She drank half a glass, then set it down and stared at the man she had consented to run away with.

Madness.

He must have sensed her mood, for he grinned and suggested she take a nap for the duration of the flight.

"You're nervous," he said.

"A little."

"You've made the right choice. There's nothing to be frightened of."

"Easy for you to say."

He laughed, and she envied him that confidence. Luke was a breed apart from most men. What he wanted, he got. What he wanted to have happen, he made happen. Still, she was nervous. There had been no talk of a deeper commitment, and Natalie knew she couldn't bear it if he decided to see other women while involved with her.

A part of her believed he wouldn't. But they had never discussed the matter. She knew the set of people Luke ran with. The rules for the rich were different.

Luke showed her to the small, comfortable bedroom aboard the plane, then left her alone as if sensing she needed some time apart from him. Natalie undressed down to her underwear, then slipped between the sheets, closed her eyes and tried to relax. But her thoughts kept coming back to Luke.

She'd learned more about him during the weeks they'd been seeing each other.

There was absolutely nothing vague about Luke. He said what he thought and laid his opinions on the line. She wouldn't have wished to change him or make him more subtle, she simply marveled at how he could be so sure of things.

The only thing she was absolutely sure of was that she never wanted to cross him or try to deceive him. She'd seen Luke in action when a business acquaintance tried to double-cross him, and Luke had been relentless in his desire for total revenge. The man hadn't even known what had hit him.

And Natalie, at that moment, had known that if she was ever in that same position, Luke would make her life a living hell.

It was best not to stand in his way.

In complete contrast to his temper, she found him to be the most sympathetic of listeners. There was no problem she wanted to discuss that he considered unimportant or small. His advice was sterling, and almost always worked. It didn't take long for Natalie to understand completely how Luke had fought his way to the top.

She felt as if her life with Luke had been destined. It had only been a matter of time before they'd headed toward the bedroom. If she'd been a smart woman and wanted a safe, predictable life with a comfortable, uncomplicated sort of man, she should have run the other way after the charity ball. She could have eventually found a man with whom she would have been quite content.

Contentment is for cows. She couldn't remember who had said that. Possibly Marta or Jane. But the statement struck her as particularly appropriate.

No, she didn't want to be simply content. She wanted to fly close to the sun, to the heart of real passion. She wanted to make love with Luke. She wanted to have the knowledge of giving herself over to this powerful man, to know what it was like to surrender herself completely.

Though Monique had never come out and said whether she approved or disapproved of Natalie's relationship with Luke, she'd helped rearrange Natalie's hectic schedule so she could take this time off. Being French, she had understood.

"There is nothing much worse in this life than for a woman's soul to be starved for passion," she'd told Natalie while they were seated in the agency's office one morning sipping coffee. "But sometimes there is a price that must be paid. Just don't expect more from this man than he is capable of giving you."

When Natalie hadn't answered, Monique had said softly, "My heart tells me that you are a woman who will someday want a family and a home. Luke is not the sort of man to give those things to you.''

Luke is not the sort of man to give those things to you.

She thought about what Monique had said as she lay in bed aboard Luke's private plane. And she found she didn't want to think further ahead than this vacation, and the closeness she and Luke would share.

She'd waited for a long time to have a sexual relationship, and was well aware that if any of her friends had been aware of her virginity they would have been astounded. At twenty-three, not many models were as innocent as she was.

But she'd wanted to wait, and had found a man who had been worth that wait. It wasn't that she hadn't been tempted. But Natalie was a woman who made decisions based almost totally on her feelings, and complete sexual intimacy with a man hadn't felt right until she'd met Luke.

That was why she'd been frightened of him, why she'd put all sorts of conditions and restraints on their relationship.

She'd known from the start that he was going to change her life forever, and she'd wanted some semblance of control over the changes.

She'd deluded herself into believing she was in control, when all the time she'd known she was dancing closer and closer to the heart of the fire.

Monique had been annoyed with her for taking six weeks off in the middle of a white-hot streak in her career, and even more frustrated when Natalie had asked her to keep her whereabouts a total secret. But there had never been a choice as far as Natalie was concerned. One thing was paramount to her. She would never sacrifice her personal life for her professional one.

It just wasn't worth it.

Natalie hadn't slept at all the night before, and the gentle vibrations of the plane combined with her own exhaustion to lull her to sleep. Just before she surrendered to it, she wondered if Luke was as deeply affected by all this as she was, or if it was business as usual for a predator.

LUKE WOKE HER as the pilot started to make his descent.

The Caribbean island of Aruba was lush and green, its hills glowing like gigantic emeralds in the midst of the brilliant blue sea. Natalie dressed quickly, then buckled herself into the seat next to Luke. He held her hand during the landing, and she sensed his awareness of her unease.

A car met them at the airport, and they drove into the hills toward the villa Luke had told her about. He'd rented it from a friend, to serve as a private retreat where they could be alone together and relax. The villa was situated overlooking the sea, with a pool that was designed so that it looked as though it had been built into the hillside.

She'd been to various parts of the Caribbean before, had traveled all over the world as a model. But she'd never been to this particular island, and she'd never traveled anywhere with Luke.

The villa was exquisite. All the large windows were open to the ocean, and lushly scented breezes cooled everything in their path. The grounds were ablaze with exotic color, well maintained and filled with brilliantly hued and gloriously scented flowers.

The slightly built man who had driven the car turned out to be an employee who lived on the premises and looked after the property when the owner wasn't around. He carried their bags into the master bedroom, then got in the car and drove down the winding hillside road.

They were alone.

"Would you like something to eat?" he asked.

Natalie shook her head. She didn't know what she wanted at the moment, but her stomach was nervous enough that she knew she didn't want to eat.

"Maybe a shower?"

That sounded good. She hoped he meant without company. Natalie knew she loved Luke, but now that the moment was at hand, she didn't want to get right down to it.

They walked into the master bedroom. The room had been painted the palest pink, the color of the inside of a seashell. The furniture was simple, painted white, and the coverlet on the king-size bed was colorful, a print in shades of turquoise, purple, peach and lime.

It was a smaller house than she'd imagined, and she liked it immediately. It had a personality of its own, that of a friendly little vacation spot, simple and serene.

Her suitcase had been placed on the big bed, and she opened it, looking for something to change into. She selected a cotton gauze caftan in a pale peach. It went with the casual atmosphere of the house, and she desperately wanted to feel more relaxed.

Gathering up shampoo, soap and body lotion, she was almost to the bathroom door when Luke's voice stopped her.

"I'm not going to simply jump your bones," he said softly. He was unpacking his clothing, arranging it in half of the large white chest of drawers on the far wall of the bedroom. "Nothing is going to happen that you don't want to have happen."

There was nothing he could have said that would have comforted her more.

"Thank you. It's just . . . hard to explain."

"No explanations necessary. It's quite a change, and from what I know about you, you don't like changes."

"No, I don't. I'll be out in a minute."

She took her time in the shower, letting the hot water relax her tense muscles. Then she dried off, rubbed jasmine-scented moisturizer into her skin and slipped the caftan over her naked body.

She found him out by the pool in a lounge chair, drink in hand. He was watching the play of sunlight on the water, and she sat down in the chair next to him.

"How are you feeling?" he asked.

"Much better."

"Would you like a drink?"

She nodded.

He brought her a glass of tropical mixed juices laced with rum. Just the thing to calm her nerves. She sipped it, studying him as she did. He'd changed from his casual clothing to a bathing suit that didn't leave a lot to the imagination. The muscles in his chest and forearms were well defined, and she could smell the scent of the sunscreen he'd applied.

"I thought we might go for a swim before dinner." They'd arrived at the island late in the afternoon, and it wouldn't be long before sunset. Darkness came suddenly in the tropics, and Natalie knew what the night would bring.

She had no doubts Luke would wait a few days if she asked him. He'd do anything in his power to make her sensual journey easier. He'd told her before, there would be no joy in the experience for him if he'd thought she'd been forced into it.

"Let's watch the sunset," she said, giving herself an emotional deadline. When the sun sank below the horizon, she would let him know the time had come.

He'd been thoughtful and patient with her, he'd protected her, looked out for her best interests.

But, above all, he was a man, and a powerful one at that. A predator. And one thing she knew was that no predator waited forever for his particular prey.

She reached for his hand and held it as she sipped her drink. The rum relaxed her, made her a little light-headed. She'd be all right. She was with Luke. More than anything, she simply wanted to let him lead, let him be the one who would ensure that her first time was absolutely wonderful.

The sun slipped lower, bathing the sky with brilliant pastels. And she sat quietly next to Luke in a comfortable silence, watching the play of color and light.

"Are we alone here?"

"Totally. No one knows where we were going except Bill, the pilot, and I trust him to be discreet."

"And the other man?" she asked, referring to the person who had picked them up at the airport.

"He's home with his family. No one knows we're here, the villa is built in a way that affords absolute privacy, and I've instructed my office not to call unless it's a true emergency."

"So even this area is private?"

"Totally."

The sun was touching the water now, shooting waves of color over the sea and bathing the sky in even deeper sunset shades.

She squeezed his hand in hers.

"I want you to know... I've never felt about any man the way I feel about you."

He tightened his fingers around hers, and the sun slipped beneath the horizon, washing the sky with a dusky light. Letting go of his hand, she stood up. Natalie moved until she was in front of his lounge chair. Her fingers went to the carved shell buttons on the shoulder of the filmy caftan. She slipped them free, then slid the garment over her shoulders until the soft peach material pooled at her feet and she was standing in front of him, completely naked.

She trembled slightly, not from any sense of cold. The tropical night was balmy, soothing and warm. She trembled because of the look in his dark eyes as he gazed at her. He lifted his arm, his hand outstretched, and she took it. He pulled her gently into his arms, and she went, glad of the emotional protection.

His arms came around her, hard and strong. Her arms twined around his neck, and she raised her face to his, wanting to lose herself in his kiss.

He kissed her, but pulled away and nuzzled her neck gently when she trembled violently.

"Natalie?"

She knew what he was asking and despised herself for being such a coward. There was only one way to get through this, and he was going to have to help her.

"Don't stop," she whispered. "I want this to happen, but it scares me at the same time. Do you understand?"

He nodded, then eased her to her feet and stood up. Taking her hand, he led her around to the far side of the pool.

She hadn't seen it before, but there was a Jacuzzi on the other side of the pool, the side that looked out over the ocean. It was cut into the mountainside, and they had to take several steps down to get to the steaming water. To their backs was black marble, gleaming darkly in the moonlight. In front of them, there was an outcropping of rocks, then sea.

"Get in," he said, and she lowered herself into the bubbling water. Luke left, and when he came back, he had their drinks.

He set both plastic glasses down next to the bubbling water, then hooked his fingers into his black suit and peeled it down his muscular legs.

She watched him, and saw him totally naked for the first time. He was a magnificent male animal, in his prime, muscled and strong. And he was most definitely aroused.

The length and strength, the sheer physical size of his sex intimidated her, and she remembered the night in Paris when she'd touched him, when he'd taught her ways to pleasure him with her hands. Since that time, he'd hardly asked for more than a kiss, keeping all passion in check for the time they'd be alone together. Within days, he'd flown her to this villa, with her seduction in mind.

He was nothing if not determined.

She caught his glance and knew he'd caught her staring. He was totally unselfconscious in his nudity, as confident as ever. He reached for her drink, handed it to her, then climbed into the Jacuzzi.

"We have all night, Natalie," he said softly as he watched her.

She swallowed several mouthfuls of the tropical drink, then set the glass down. She'd never tire of looking at him, the sharp planes of his face, the fiercely possessive glow in his eyes, the powerful muscles in his shoulders and arms. He was hers, for tonight, for as many nights thereafter as he wanted her.

She didn't want to think of what the future might bring, what kind of heartache might be in store. She only wanted this man, this moment, this night. If nothing else happened afterward, she would have passionate memories to warm the rest of her life.

Natalie wanted to know what lovemaking could entail, and she wanted to learn from a man who brought out feelings deep inside her no one else had even touched. Knowing Luke had made her curious about the ecstasy a woman could achieve in a man's arms.

Though she was still a little frightened of him, she didn't want to play it safe her first time. She'd waited for a man like Luke, and now the time had come.

"Make love to me," she whispered, knowing she wanted to give him everything a woman could give a man she loved.

He approached her with a fluid, liquid grace, moving toward her, a relentless male animal. Before she could draw another breath, she felt his body pinning hers against the smooth expanse of black marble at her back. Then he was kissing her with a hunger that told her what his control had cost him.

It shocked her, this much raw sexual feeling in a single kiss. She whimpered against his lips and felt the powerful shudder that shook his masculine body.

Patience had taken its toll on her predator.

His fingers were threaded through her wet hair, tilting her head as his mouth covered hers.

Her eyes had been half-closed, and now they drifted shut as she slid her hands up his arms to his shoulders then into his hair. There was a demand in his kiss, one she was powerless to refuse. With instinctive ease, she opened her mouth to his, letting him deepen the kiss and take her closer to passion's fire.

Skin touched skin, and even through the heat of the bubbling water and despite the hot steam that surrounded them, she could feel the sexual heat that emanated from his hair-roughened body. There wasn't an inch of her body that wasn't exposed to him, that wasn't open to him, that he couldn't caress.

His hand closed over her breast almost roughly, but she didn't cry out. She'd pushed him to the brink of patience, and she wanted to experience a part of the passion she'd unleashed. She felt him catch her nipple between his thumb and forefinger, and she arched into the sensation as he lowered his mouth to her breasts.

She felt the roughness of his tongue as it flicked over her nipple, then he was suckling strongly, his cheeks flexing. She heard a cry, as if from a distance, and realized it was her own voice, her own needs being given primitive expression. But no one could hear her, no one could see what was happening between them. They were totally alone, and she felt as if she'd unleashed a tiger.

His hand slipped between her legs, and she knew he could feel the burning wetness as he slowly eased a finger inside her. He stroked her, heightening her pleasure until her whimpers turned to sharp cries, then low moans of pleasure.

She rocked her hips against his hand, taking pleasure from him, urging him on. She felt as if she was totally out of control, and she knew the exact moment when she gave over to his possession completely.

He lifted her out of the Jacuzzi and lowered her to the wet marble, his hot, hard body slipping between her thighs and pinning her to the cool, smooth surface. Several tiny waterfalls had been built into the wall behind them, and she could feel the warm mist covering her body with a fine sheen.

He was breathing deeply as he looked down at her. She couldn't take her eyes off him. Something in his expression shifted, and she glanced at what had caught his attention. He was staring at her upper thigh, and she saw the red mark on her fair skin where he'd gripped her tightly.

She hadn't even felt it.

At the same moment, she felt him denying himself the violently sexual emotions that had surrounded them mere seconds ago. Instinctively, she knew he didn't think her capable of taking in all the passion he was capable of giving her. Reacting out of a purely primitive, feminine need, she reached up and hooked her hand around his neck, bringing his face toward hers.

"Don't," she whispered, fighting the way pure, hot excitement caused her throat to close. "I want it all, everything you're capable of giving me. I want to do everything with you. Don't hold back, Luke. *Please.* You won't hurt me."

She sensed the struggle he was having with his control. If he did what instinct told him to do, he would bring her to ground in a blaze of passion, like a predator racing after its prey and finally consuming it. If he did what he thought best for her, he would temper his actions and wait until he decided she was ready for more.

She forced her lips to mouth the words as they brushed his ear. "Make love to me the way you really want to. The way I know you want to...."

He caught fire again, her words proving too irresistible a temptation. He pressed himself along the length of her body, and she felt his hard, hot shaft against her belly, almost burning the sensitive skin. Then he was moving down her body, kissing, caressing, biting softly.

Staking the most primitive and sensual of claims.

She gasped at the assault on her senses, then grasped his head as he slowly and relentlessly teased her with his kisses. Her breasts, her belly, her inner thighs. Then he pushed her thighs apart and kissed the very heart of her, causing her hips to buck upward in sensual surprise.

She'd never been kissed there before, and she felt he was deflowering her with his mouth. He licked and sucked and bit until she was sobbing, the breath catching in her throat, the level of sensual frustration at its peak.

He slid up her body with a fierceness that thrilled her and thrust into her virginal sheath with one swift stroke, forcing himself past the barrier that proclaimed her innocence. The pain was sharp and intense as he took her, but she simply held on to his shoulders tightly as sensation claimed her. Emotions overflowed within her and she started to cry, silently, as he rocked against her and made her his own.

It was a fierce coupling, and she knew what it was like to be in a predator's arms. He took her with a savagery that stunned her, swept her into a maelstrom of passion that carried her higher and higher.

He'd made her climax before, and she recognized the sensations foreshadowing the moment. And despite his fierceness, despite the way he'd taken her, she felt safe in his arms, safe enough to simply give over and let him have the darkest, most secret part of herself.

Her climax triggered his, and she was stunned by the force and beauty of his release. She lay beneath him, panting, her body filled with a fine, exhausted trembling. Tears flowed silently out of her eyes, and as she raised her hand and gently stroked his dark hair, her heart was filled with joy that it had been this man who had taken her virginity, this man who had introduced her to her sensual side.

After what might have been a minute or an hour, he lifted himself up off her, resting his weight on his elbows but keeping her pinned beneath him. He noticed her tears immediately, and she recognized deep concern in his eyes.

"No," she whispered, touching his cheek. "No, it's not because you hurt me...."

He must have understood how she was feeling, because he gathered her into his arms and rolled to his side, uncoupling their bodies but keeping her pressed tightly against him.

"Natalie," he whispered, and she put her finger to his lips.

"Perfect," she whispered, then fell asleep.

SHE WOKE INSIDE THE bedroom, beneath the covers. The room was very dark, and she sensed his presence next to her. His body gave off masculine heat and warmed the bed they both lay in.

She didn't move, had only opened her eyes, yet he knew she was awake. She sensed it.

He moved his hand between her legs, cupping her, covering her mound. She felt tender, but didn't push his hand away. She couldn't.

And it was at that moment that she recognized the extent of his power over her.

With his other hand, he encircled her waist and pulled her against him so her back rested against his front. He kissed the back of her neck and she shivered, feeling the hot length of his arousal against her buttocks.

She thought about whispering to him and found she didn't want to talk. She wanted to feel. The room was dark, they were all alone in the world, he was strongly aroused, and she wanted to follow this erotic pathway of desire and see where it would lead.

She trusted him. He wouldn't hurt her. He would only give to her. She'd told him she wanted to explore all of it with him, at the Jacuzzi, and he was obviously taking her at her word.

I want to do everything with you....

She placed her hand over his, pressing it against her tender flesh, and he began to move his fingers, rubbing, caressing, slipping them inside her heat. She responded, moving against his hand, turning her head so she could kiss his lips fleetingly.

He readied her slowly, carefully, until she was twisting and writhing against the cool white sheets in a frenzy of sexual frustration. Her rational thought process seemed to have shut down, and the wisdom of her body, ancient and primal, had taken over.

There was nothing he couldn't have done to her in that dark bedroom.

He pleasured her until she cried out and buried her face against the pillow. Until she found her release against that relentlessly knowing hand.

GET A FREE TEDDY BEAR...

You'll love this plush, cuddly Teddy Bear, an adorable accessory for your dressing table, bookcase or desk. Measuring 5½" tall, he's soft and brown and has a bright red ribbon around his neck—he's completely captivating! And he's yours *absolutely free*, when you accept this no-risk offer!

He knew how to make it so good for her. He knew what she wanted, how to touch, how to move, what to whisper, how to make her feel as if she'd never inhabited her body before.

As if she'd never been truly alive before.

Sensuality consumed her as he kept her on the brink of release, then moved slowly up her body until his lips grazed her ear.

His whispered words were rough, dark and erotic.

She couldn't resist him, or anything he wanted to do. She kissed him, moaning deep in her throat as she did, and felt his lips, hard and assured, against hers. He bit the side of her neck, guided her with his hands.

She might have been innocent, but she was quick to learn. Whatever he wanted, she wanted to give.

His masculine penetration was exquisite, deep and strong and sure. He moved his knee slightly, forcing her legs farther apart, letting him sink deeper inside her.

There would be no holding back with this man. Ever. Whatever he wanted, he would find a way to get, for he was just as ruthless in bed as out of it.

He caressed her, and she felt her climax racing toward her, then she couldn't feel anything but her own shattering release.

When she could think clearly again, she was lying on her side and he was next to her, his hand gently stroking the hair out of her eyes.

"Luke..."

He kissed her into silence. She touched him, and found from her exploration of his body that he hadn't found satisfaction yet.

"Luke," she whispered, her hand closing around the hardness between his muscled thighs.

He told her what he wanted, his words explicit. She kissed him as he rolled onto his back, then he helped her straddle him, then sink down on his hardness, taking it inside her, stroking him, moving on him, arousing him even further.

They moved slowly, leisurely. She listened to the sound of his breathing, touched his hair-roughened chest, marveled at the way his muscles jumped at her touch. More confident with this much control, she leaned down and kissed one of his nipples, then took it into her mouth and suckled strongly, as he had done to her.

She wanted to give him everything, make him hers, ensure that he'd never forget this night or have the desire for anyone else in this lifetime.

His hands tightened on her buttocks and his breathing deepened. She could make out his face in the darkness, and she leaned over him, capturing his lips with hers.

Fearless, no longer afraid of anything that could happen between them, she rocked harder and harder as sensation quickened inside her. She felt his shaft harden even more, then he was holding her hips in a painful grip and thrusting up, again and again, until that last shuddering thrust told her he'd reached completion.

She slid down on top of him, feeling boneless and weightless and so very cherished. She kissed him, hard, nipped his bottom lip, then exhausted all over again, fell promptly asleep.

THEY DIDN'T LEAVE the villa's grounds for the entire six weeks.

It was as if they couldn't get enough of each other. She even stopped bothering with clothes. She remembered her frustrations while packing, told him, and he laughed. She'd been right—he wouldn't have cared if she hadn't brought any clothing at all.

They sunbathed, swam, made love, ate, made love, slept, walked on the beach, made love—and stayed within constant reach of each other.

It frightened her, how she didn't miss any of her old life. There were times she could barely remember it. All he had to do was look at her, touch her a certain way, and her body came alive.

She was the most willing of erotic students, and he was the most able of teachers. There wasn't a sexual path they didn't explore, and each encounter only served to make her want him more. She felt as if she belonged to him, and that in giving to him, she was the one who received.

The feeling was obviously reciprocated.

He considered her his now, and that knowledge brought her pleasure. Though she knew many of her female friends would have thought her feelings were hopelessly outdated, she wanted Luke to be the strong one in their relationship, she wanted him to take control. She loved the way he made love to her, and she wanted nothing in the realm of the senses to be off limits to either of them.

They talked far into the night. She told him of her parents' divorce, her grandmother's death and her mother's subsequent breakdowns. He listened as no one else ever had, and with his arms around her, she felt safe and protected.

He didn't offer up much about his past, and she respected his desire for privacy. She knew he wasn't particularly close to his family, but that he adored his sister. But they grew closer to each other with each revelation, with each sensual encounter, with moments spent together away from the world.

All too soon, it was time to leave. The night before their departure, they sat out by the pool and watched another sunset.

Natalie took Luke's hand in her own, then kissed his palm.

"Thank you."

"For what?"

"This island. This time together. For making everything so special."

"Thank you for being willing to come with me."

They were sharing a chaise longue, and she leaned back and, her heart in her throat, whispered words that came from her soul.

"I'll never love anyone the way I love you, Luke."

His arms tightened around her, but he said nothing in return. Her eyes stung at her own foolishness. She'd said the words on impulse, had told herself it wouldn't matter if he didn't respond in kind. But it did matter, desperately, and if she could have called those words back, she would have.

Luke was a man who could have any woman in the world. Why would he even think of loving just one?

He kissed the top of her head, and she felt hot tears stand out in her eyes. Desperate not to cry in front of him, she blinked furiously.

"Natalie."

He touched her chin, tried to turn her head toward him, but she stubbornly refused.

"Natalie."

Her tears under control, she looked at him.

And if she lived forever, she'd never forget the expression on his face. Tenderness, passion—and a touch of wonder.

"I love you."

She couldn't speak. She felt as if the wildly violent part of his nature, the predator, had simply lain down at her feet and rolled over onto its back in total submission.

She'd submitted to him in coming to this island, and that submission had reached its deepest moments within the confines of their bedroom. Now, in a different way and at a different time, he was reciprocating.

In daring to ride the tiger, she'd tamed him and made him her own.

She knew how vulnerable the declaration made him. It thrilled her as nothing else in her life ever had. And she realized, from a place within her heart, that she would never use his feelings for her against him.

She'd never want to.

"Oh, Luke," she breathed, then shifted her body so she turned toward him, embraced him, surrendered herself to the warmth and strength of his arms.

They lay on the chaise, arms tightly entwined, long after the sun disappeared into the sea.

Chapter Seven

On their third day in Fairplay, Luke and Natalie finally made it to the Golden Nugget Café for lunch.

The Nugget, as it was called by the locals, was Mae Crawford's pride and joy. The townspeople teased Otis about his marriage to Mae, telling him that the only reason he'd gotten hitched to her was that she was such an excellent cook.

Otis's long hours working on the trail, coupled with Cookie's lousy trail food, had whetted his appetite for a decent meal. It was said once he'd met Mae and tasted her fried chicken, Otis hadn't stood a chance.

Luke opened the door of the small café for Natalie, then stepped in after her. It was a cheerful place, warm and friendly.

The floors were tongue-in-groove pine boards that Otis had found in an old barn and refinished. The tables and chairs were of all sizes and styles, but all of them were wooden. A large black potbellied stove stood in the center of the eating area, with a few comfortable, overstuffed chairs placed around it. Bright red and white gingham curtains were at the double-paned windows, and the walls were filled to bursting with all sorts of relics and artifacts.

There were a lot of framed pictures hanging on the log walls, from early photos of miners and settlers to current pictures of town celebrations. The picture frames were a haphazard lot, but somehow Mae had managed to blend the whole into a satisfying decor.

And even if the surroundings might not have encouraged a customer to step inside, his first sniff of what Mae had cooking would have been a surefire lure.

No nouvelle cuisine here, Luke thought. From what Natalie had told him, Fairplay still possessed and cherished its frontier spirit. The Nugget's fare reflected this attitude. Typical of its menu were items like chili or beans, steak and squaw bread, biscuits and gravy. Corn bread and dumplings and rolls. Cobblers and crisps, fritters and pies.

Everything was from scratch, nothing from a mix. Mae was a truly formidable cook, and it was her recipes and her energetic spirit that made the Nugget the success it was.

There was no need to wait for someone to show them to a table, so Luke followed Natalie to a table for two by one of the windows. The menus were already on the tables, along with salt, sugar, pepper, a napkin dispenser and a bottle of Tabasco sauce.

He pulled out her chair for her, then sat down across from her and reached for one of the menus.

But his attention was on Natalie.

She looked even better today. They'd slept in pretty late, then walked to the Nugget for lunch. The brisk autumn wind had whipped a little color into her cheeks. He'd insisted that she dress warmly, and she'd paired a long denim skirt with a denim shirt, an oversize raspberry sweater and cowboy boots. He'd just pulled on his jeans, a denim shirt, his boots and a black sweatshirt.

Her long, dark hair was braided down her back, and she hadn't put on any makeup at all, but to Luke she was still the prettiest woman in the room. In the world.

"What'll it be?" the waitress asked. She was a tall, angular redhead with freckles, dressed in jeans and a green cotton shirt.

"Hi, Cora," Natalie said.

"Well, Natalie, I didn't even recognize you! And this must be Luke."

Introductions were made, then their order taken. Cora scribbled it down rapidly on her pad, talking the entire time.

"Mae'll be out of the kitchen the minute she knows you're here. How long are you planning on staying?"

"Just a few more days."

"Glad to have you back." She briskly brought Luke some coffee, then headed toward the kitchen with their order.

True to Cora's word, Mae appeared within minutes. A tall woman, with high cheekbones and silvery hair pulled back in a soft bun, she walked right up to their table and, when Natalie stood up, enfolded her in a hug.

"Otis told me you were in town. I figured you'd make your way down here sooner or later. And this must be your nice young man...."

Luke stood, smiled and shook her hand. He was beginning to get used to the genuine friendliness of Fairplay's people, and found it a refreshing change from what he usually dealt with in business.

"Now, honey," Mae said, all concern as she addressed Natalie while she and Luke sat down, "I know you ordered the turkey, but I have to tell you that the chili is something special today. You won't be sorry if you order it."

Luke watched as Natalie's hand went to her stomach and she explained to Mae that she'd been having some trouble with it. The older woman's expression grew worried.

"In that case, you stick to your order. I made some custard, fresh this morning, and it'll be just the thing for dessert, nice and bland."

"That does sound good."

"And you ordered the steak, Luke, but I'll bring you a bowl of red on the house, how's that?"

He couldn't help smiling at the woman's enthusiasm. He liked people who were passionate about their work, and Mae was certainly passionate about the food at the Nugget.

"Sounds good."

Mae had barely bustled off when the front door swung open, the attached cowbells jangling noisily. Otis entered, followed by two other men. One, of medium height and skinny as a rail, was followed by a little boy. The other, short, stout and almost completely bald, brought up the rear.

"What happened to the pumpkin, Grandpa?" the boy asked. He looked to be about five and had thick blond hair and inquisitive brown eyes.

"Couldn't use it as a jack-o'-lantern," the skinny man replied. "Why, it was so big, we hollowed it out and used it as the town meetin' hall for a number of years."

Otis caught Luke's eye, and the entire party headed toward their table.

"Hello to you both," he said. "Natalie, good to see you up and about."

"You know I can't resist Mae's cooking," she replied. "That fried chicken the other night was the best."

"Ah, Otis'll keep her around," said the skinny man before thrusting his hand out to Luke. "Name's Pete." He indicated the stout man with a wave of his hand. "That's Sam, and this here's my grandson, Mike."

"Would you like to join us?" Natalie asked. "We just came in to have lunch."

"Think you can stand this little ruffian?" Pete asked, ruffling his grandson's hair.

"I think we can manage it," Luke replied.

They moved to a larger table.

"Think the chili's good today?" Sam asked as he perused the menu.

"It'll put some hair on your chest," Cora said from behind Sam, making him jump.

"It's hair on his head he's needing," Otis said, then leaned back as Sam tried to swat him with the menu.

"I'll have chili and a beer," said Pete.

"Bowl o' red sounds good," seconded Otis. "And a beer."

"I want a piece of cake," Mike chimed in. "The chocolate one."

"And I suppose you want a beer, too?" Cora asked Mike and winked. "I'll make it a root beer."

"He already had two corn dogs down at the J Bar J," Pete said. "It's a wonder he don't explode, the food this little varmint eats."

"I'll have biscuits and gravy, with a side order of ham," said Sam. "And save me one of them doughnuts. Pick me a fresh one, Cora."

"Will do, handsome." She finished writing their orders with a flourish, then headed toward the kitchen.

Luke felt the tiniest bit like an outsider, but Natalie seemed happy to see the three old men, so he sat back and decided to enjoy lunch.

"Can I sit next to you?" Mike asked Natalie.

"Sure."

He changed seats with Pete, then continued to stare.

"You sure are pretty," the little boy said.

"He's a wild one when it comes to women," Otis said, grinning at Luke. "Just like his grandpa."

"Now, cut that out," Pete replied good-naturedly. "He sees a pretty little filly and he speaks his mind. No shame in that."

"We're looking for Seldom," Mike told Natalie, his manner grave.

"Seldom?" she asked. "What's that?"

"Grandpa's dog."

"His name is Seldom?" asked Luke. He was beginning to get the rhythm of this conversation, and surprised to find that he liked it—and just about understood it.

"Seldom Fed," Mike said.

Luke choked on his coffee, and Otis good-naturedly pounded him on the back. Once his coughing subsided and his eyes stopped watering, the conversation resumed.

"We couldn't find him this morning," Mike said. "He didn't come in for breakfast."

"And the way that dog loves to eat, you know something's wrong," Pete said.

They discussed various ideas as to where Seldom might be hiding out. Luke and Natalie's lunch came, and the three older men told them to go right ahead and eat. It wasn't that much later that the rest of the orders were delivered to the table.

"Best ham in town," Sam said, cutting himself a generous slice. "I ordered some ham in a café in a town that shall remain nameless, but that piece of meat smelled strong enough to perform the labors of Hercules.''

They enjoyed the meal, talking and laughing. Natalie was eating her custard and Luke and the men were all enjoying fresh apple pie and hot coffee when they heard a crash outside, followed by Mae's voice hollering curses.

''Pete!'' She strode into the café, soupspoon in hand and green eyes flashing. ''Get that renegade dog o' yours out of my garbage or I'm gonna get my shotgun!''

''Seldom!'' Mike shouted, sliding out of his chair and running toward the back door of the restaurant.

''I'll take care of it, Mae.'' Pete stood up, turned toward Natalie and took her hand. ''Much obliged, ma'am, for having lunch with us. I hope I'll see you again before you leave for Denver.''

''Thanks, Pete.''

Luke didn't miss the genuine affection all three men had for Natalie, nor the enjoyment she seemed to derive from their company. She looked happier, more relaxed than she had in a long time, and he decided they were both going to make the time to get away to Fairplay more often.

THEY TOOK A DRIVE to a secluded meadow and walked for a while, looking at the brilliant leaves turning on the trees. Luke had brought a blanket, and when they stopped to rest, he spread it at the edge of the meadow and they lay down on it.

"I like being lazy," Natalie announced. She was lying with her head in his lap, and he was playing with her braid.

"You should do it more often. It helps you keep that edge."

"Luke, where do you see yourself in ten years?"

He sensed the importance of the question and didn't hesitate with his answer.

"With you."

"What else?"

He could have told her exactly where he wanted the business to be, but he knew that wasn't what she was asking him. As for his personal life, as long as she was by his side, he had no complaints.

"I hadn't really thought about it." He didn't want to say the wrong thing and upset her, and he wasn't sure where this conversation was going. It made him uneasy, not being in control, and he decided to turn the tables.

"What about you?"

"I don't think I'll be modeling anymore."

"You'd only be thirty-seven. There are a lot of women in their thirties still in the business."

"Not me."

He thought of Monique Devereux. "What about running your own agency?"

"No."

"Tell me what you want to be doing."

The answer seemed to hover on the tip of her tongue, then she sighed and said, "I'm not really sure.

The only thing I'm sure of is that I want to be with you."

"Then," he said, sliding down so they were lying side by side on the blanket and he could take her in his arms, "I don't think we have anything to worry about."

SHE WENT TO BED EARLY that night, after eating some of the chicken and dumplings Mae sent over. Luke sat in the living room, made several calls to check on various business deals, then lay on the couch and wondered if he'd tired her out.

Her improvement seemed to be erratic. They might have to stay here longer than a week. Within a week and a half, he'd have to make a quick trip into Denver, but he could trust Otis and Mae to keep an eye on Natalie.

The soft knock on the door roused him out of his thoughts, and he swung his long legs off the sofa, strode to the door and opened it.

Doc Harte stood on the front porch, his black bag in his hand.

"I was just over at the Hadley place, checking up on Sally and her new baby. I thought I'd stop by and see how Natalie was getting on."

"She's asleep." Noticing that Doc looked tired, Luke stepped aside and motioned for him to enter.

"Coffee?"

"That would be appreciated."

The two men headed toward the kitchen. Luke fixed a pot of coffee, then rummaged through the refrigerator until he found the leftover apple pie from dinner. He cut Doc a generous slice, then warmed it up in the microwave.

"You look like you could use some rest yourself."

Doc nodded, then took his hat off and set it on the table. "Babies can be exhausting. Sally's had a difficult time with this one."

"What happened?"

Doc explained while he ate his pie and drank his coffee, but the entire time Luke felt as though something else was going on below the surface. As if he was being tested by this wise old man. Those eyes of his had seen more than he was letting on, and Luke decided the best approach was a direct one.

"There's something Natalie isn't telling me."

"That's a fact." Doc set down his coffee cup with a soft thump. He'd eaten all his pie, down to the last flaky piece of crust. "But I don't intend to get between the two of you and cause any trouble. Anything that girl wants to tell you, she's going to have to tell you herself."

"Is it serious?"

"I'd say so."

"Is she . . . is it—"

"Nothing life-threatening, if that's what you mean." He held up a hand. "No, no more questions. It's best if she tells you herself. Don't push her, she's the sort that needs a little time. I've seen it happen this way before. You're doing the best thing for her, Luke, simply letting her have some peace and quiet and staying close to her side.''

The grandfather clock in the hallway ticked quietly as he studied Doc, trying to figure out what the older man could be talking about.

''You love her, don't you?'' Doc asked quietly.

Luke wouldn't have answered that question for any other man, but his respect for Doc was instinctive.

''Yes.''

''Then everything will be fine. Don't worry, son, these things have a way of working themselves out.'' He reached for his hat, then his jacket, then his black bag.

''The coffee and pie were much appreciated. I have two more stops to make before I can go home, and it was just the thing to keep my stomach from growling.'' He smiled, an easy, friendly smile, and Luke found himself responding in kind.

He walked Doc to the front door, and as the older man was leaving he turned toward Luke and offered one last piece of advice.

''There's a dance at the J Bar J Saturday night. I don't know about you, but I've noticed that most women like to go to dances now and again. You might ask her.''

It was beyond thinking about, Doc Harte advising him on his love life.

''Thanks, Doc. I'll do that.''

He watched Doc from the front door, then the window as the older man made his way steadily down the street.

So I wasn't imagining it.

There was something else going on, something Natalie still didn't feel she could share with him. They'd been together almost four years, and he hadn't thought they had any more secrets from each other. It hurt, to find out that she thought she couldn't trust him with this.

Even if Doc hadn't come right out and said it, Luke would have known he couldn't push Natalie into telling him. He'd simply have to stay close to her and make sure the opportunity arose.

NATALIE CREPT UP the stairway on silent bare feet. She'd started downstairs when she'd heard Doc talking to Luke, then frozen on the stairway when she'd overheard parts of their conversation.

Doc had kept his promise, but she'd been foolish enough to believe Luke wouldn't know something was wrong. He'd always been a mind reader when it came to her, could always tell when something was bothering her or someone had upset her.

She'd been happy he was so perceptive, as a great deal of the time that masculine perception had been used to keep her happy. Now, when she saw her future stretched out in front of her, her life without Luke, she wished he was a little less perceptive so they might have a little more time together.

Slipping up the stairs, she retreated into the master bathroom.

It was time to rethink the entire situation.

The bathroom had a large, Victorian-style tub and a pedestal sink. She'd also moved in a large chest of drawers to contain all the things that usually cluttered up medicine chests and shelves.

Now, she opened up one of the drawers and took out a bottle of lavender-scented bath gel. Turning on the water in the tub full force, she squeezed the bottle, and a froth of cleanly scented bubbles began to fill the tub.

She slipped off her nightgown and robe and hung them up on one of the pegs on the closed door. Usually, she didn't shut the bathroom door when she bathed, and many nights Luke came home from work to find her resting in the tub after a particularly hard day at work.

He'd never been what she considered a shy man, and they'd had some of their best talks in the bathroom. He'd bring in a bottle of wine, pour two glasses, and more often than not join her in the tub.

But tonight she needed some time alone. She had to think about what she was going to do. Originally, she'd thought she might have some of that time by herself in Fairplay, but that wasn't the case. She really hadn't expected Luke to come up after her, though she had been deeply moved that he had.

He knew something was really wrong.

She studied her body, and the subtle changes the pregnancy had made, in the large, free-standing mirror. She couldn't keep her pregnancy a secret from Luke much longer. He had too sharp an eye.

Her breasts were larger. The morning sickness didn't show, physically, but Luke would soon start to wonder at all the mornings she spent hiding in the bathroom.

Turning away from the mirror, she got into the tub, leaning back so her neck rested comfortably on the tub's rolled edge. The water was almost as high as she wanted it, so she waited just a little longer, then turned it off.

The cabin was silent. Luke was probably still downstairs. If he saw that the bathroom door was shut, he wouldn't come in.

She closed her eyes, contemplating her dilemma in the total silence of the house. The logs provided excellent insulation from noise, and Fairplay wasn't all that loud a town to begin with, except for holidays. Part of what she'd sought coming here was peace, and she'd found it.

But peace within herself—that was the hard part.

More than anything, she didn't want to give Luke the impression that she had all the answers. That she'd already made all the decisions. She'd wanted, more than anything, for them to make decisions regarding this baby together, like a married couple.

But they weren't married. She'd known, early on, that Luke had been married before and the relationship had been disastrous. His ex had bled him for every cent she could, so when marriage had come up as a subject between them, he'd asked her to sign a prenuptial agreement.

She'd been quietly furious, and told him that in that case, she had no further interest in getting married to him. She'd live with him as his lover, and they'd keep their money separate, thank you very much.

Easy words for an independent woman to say. Not so easy, never so simple, when a child was involved.

Luke had also told her that he didn't consider himself to be a family man, and she'd remembered Monique's warning words to her that day at the agency. She'd asked him why, and he'd told her there were two reasons he felt that way.

First, he hadn't grown up with the greatest of examples and he'd botched his one attempt at marriage. She'd sensed instinctively that he was a man who found losing at anything an abhorrently painful experience.

And second, he'd grown sick of all the women who'd, after a first or second date, blithely announced that their biological clock was running out and they wanted marriage and a baby, boom, just like that.

They'd been sharing dinner at a tiny French bistro in New York and she remembered setting her salad fork down and leaning closer toward him, feeling his pain.

They'd seen him as a commodity.

"I can understand that," she'd told him.

"You can?" he'd answered warily.

"Certainly. Because they didn't say the most important, necessary thing."

"And what's that?" His tone had been slightly sarcastic, but it hadn't bothered her. She'd known, deep inside, what he was feeling.

"They didn't say that they wanted to get married to *you,* or that they wanted to have *your* baby." Calmly, having dropped her little bomb, she picked up her wineglass and took a sip.

He'd eyed her with a disturbingly intent expression on his face.

"Don't start making me into something I'm not, Natalie," he said finally, his voice very quiet and controlled. "I've never promised you what I don't believe I'm capable of giving."

"I know," she'd replied. "But I have a right to my own opinion, and even though you may dislike hearing it, I think you'd make a terrific husband. I know I don't think I could find anyone better."

He hadn't been happy with the conversation. Luke Garner felt more at home in the world of business, where he could remain in control. He wasn't as comfortable around deep emotion, which was where she liked to live.

How they had ever lasted this long was a miracle to her. But maybe love was the miracle. And maybe love could work just one more in her favor....

Closing her eyes, she concentrated on relaxing, and wondered how on earth she was going to tell him he'd be a father next spring.

HE HEARD the bathwater running, and knew the door would be closed. And he remembered other baths, other times and places, and yearned for the closeness they'd had before.

He'd gone over everything, every clue, over and over again since Doc had left. And he didn't know what to do, other than give her a little more time and hope that she would confide in him soon.

It didn't suit him in the slightest, being inactive. He liked to make things happen, not wait for them to unfold. He could be patient in a business deal and stalk someone with the utmost skill, but in matters of the heart he liked to know exactly where he stood.

He liked to be in control.

He couldn't think of anything she'd be that frightened to tell him. All he knew, with utter certainty, was that she was uncertain of his commitment to her. Otherwise, she would have already confided in him.

The house was completely silent, and he marveled at the quiet that he felt right down to his bones. How could he be in such a peaceful, restful place and feel more agitated than he ever had in his entire life?

He listened as she turned on the taps again, probably adding a little more hot water to her bath. And he thought of climbing the stairs, opening the bathroom door, stripping his clothes off and joining her in that hot water.

A temporary solution to a problem that was threatening to become permanent.

He thought of what he wished he could tell her, trying to put his feelings into words.

Trust me, Natalie. Believe in me, in us. I have strength enough for both of us, if you'll only believe it.

But he knew her temperament and her various moods. If he asked her to tell him what was wrong, she'd only retreat into her shell. Advance and retreat. The relationship dance. Her moods were maddening, but he'd have to wait this particular one out.

Unable to get his mind off the woman upstairs, Luke wondered what he could possibly do to make her feel safe.

He took a deep breath, then rubbed his fingers against the bridge of his nose. He was on the way to the downstairs bathroom to look for some aspirin when the solution hit him.

Within seconds, he was on the phone to Peter, his assistant, giving him careful instructions concerning a certain jeweler in New York. As long as the engagement ring was here by Saturday night, the date of his and Natalie's four-year anniversary, things would go smoothly. Just as he planned they would.

It was all so very simple.

He would insure that his future included Natalie by asking her to be his wife. And she would feel safer within their relationship with the security of marriage.

This time, he wouldn't bother with a prenuptial agreement. It had been a foolish request the first time, and Natalie had been quietly enraged. But he'd been burned badly by his ex-wife, and thought it necessary. He hadn't been thinking clearly. He'd still been licking his financial wounds.

Natalie, though her moods could be thoroughly frustrating and incomprehensible, had brought him nothing but joy in the years he'd been with her.

Luke smiled, his hand still on the phone receiver he'd hung up.

He'd ask Natalie to marry him.

And this time, he wouldn't take no for an answer.

Chapter Eight

She never spent another night in her apartment after they returned from the Caribbean.

Arrangements were never discussed, she simply moved in with Luke. Feelings and emotions ran high, and neither of them wanted to be apart more than was necessary.

She packed a suitcase with essentials, but Luke made all the arrangements for the move. She didn't have a great deal, mostly books, artwork and a few pieces of furniture. She'd always loved plants and animals, but had been reluctant to have either when she was away as often as she was and couldn't give them the attention they deserved.

Natalie knew what people were going to say, and what she would eventually become in their eyes. But none of it mattered. The only thing that mattered was that she was with Luke and both of them were happy.

Two years after their first meeting at the charity ball in New York, she was one of the most successful models in the city. There wasn't an assignment she wasn't offered, and her price was high. Monique Devereux had helped shape her career brilliantly, and Luke had been there for each step taken, his advice offered only when she asked for it. He'd been supportive of her dreams, and that had meant a lot to her.

Today, they were shooting a fashion spread for a major magazine in Vermont, the models posing against blazing, brilliant foliage. Mick Lewis was the principle photographer on the shoot, and both Jane and Marta, her closest friends in the business, were on assignment, as well.

They broke for lunch. Mick had become something of a superstar in the world of fashion photography and traveled with quite an entourage. Taking a tip from Maurice Kouris, he'd brought along his own chef. Being English, Mick was used to operating in an American manner, but as he was getting older, he'd become obsessed with the effects of stress on his system.

Thus, Mick now lived his life in a more Mediterranean manner. Long lunches. Freshly cooked foods, with the emphasis on fruits and vegetables. He'd read a study that claimed moderate drinking was good for the heart, and considered his two glasses of red wine, one with lunch and another with dinner, to be medicinal rather than alcoholic.

This suited everyone on the shoot. They were ahead of schedule, so when Mick called a lunch break, everyone was looking forward to whatever gourmet delicacy his chef had managed to prepare. Serge was a genius with food, and could work anywhere. Today, his kitchen was a farmhouse on the property where they were shooting.

The meal was simple, asparagus rice soup, a large salad and grilled salmon. Natalie had just finished preparing her plate from the generous buffet and was heading toward the large pine table when she noticed Jane stuffing a newspaper into her tote bag.

"What's that?" she said as she sat down. Mick joined them, carrying two bottles of red wine.

Marta had already started eating. She'd caught pneumonia the year before, and her career had suffered for it. Natalie had talked Mick into helping Marta get this job. It was a plum assignment and would help her move her career up to where she'd been before she'd been sick.

"Nothing," Jane replied, her usually animated face averted.

"She's going to see it sooner or later, it may as well be sooner," Mick said, as he poured himself a glass of wine and started the bottle around the table.

"What?"

Jane glared at Mick, then pulled out the crumpled newspaper. Natalie recognized the lurid colors and huge, bold headlines of one of the tabloids.

And she was on the cover.

They hadn't had to crop the photograph, put her head on someone else's body or position her so she was next to another picture of Luke. They'd been leaving a movie theater, arms around each other, and his head had been bent toward hers.

She even remembered the moment the paparazzo had taken the photo, the flash of light, Luke's sudden annoyance, his arm coming up to protect her and ward off any more shots.

Neither of them were naive about the press, and they usually posed for pictures if asked. It was part of being in the public eye. But neither of them particularly cared for being surprised by a blinding flash.

She studied the tabloid. The headline read, "Top Model Became Millionaire's Mistress to Advance Career." Ignoring her lunch, Natalie scanned the newspaper, looking for the article.

"Don't let your food get cold over something like this," Mick advised.

"Natalie, don't," Jane said quietly. "It's just garbage."

But it was addictive garbage, especially when she'd seen her own picture, and Luke's, on the cover. The article boasted a few more photos of the two of them together, and a glamour shot of her alone. The entire piece ran two pages, and "a good friend" was the source of most of the information.

Finished, she set the tabloid down and picked up her glass of wine.

"Here's to the press," she said, forcing a smile. This was a crucial assignment, to both Mick and herself, let alone Jane and Marta. She wasn't going to let her mood bring everyone down. Natalie had been around enough temperamental models who'd made everyone's lives miserable, and she'd been determined from the start of her career that she'd never be like them.

"I'm sorry, Natalie," Jane said quietly. "I didn't mean for you to see it."

"It's okay." And it was, she decided. She wouldn't let it touch her. Nothing could touch her, as long as she was with Luke.

She couldn't have known it at that time, but much later she realized she'd been flying too close to the sun.

THE STRESS AT THE TOP began to affect her.

Or, as Luke insisted, she let it affect her.

"Don't think about these people," he said one evening after catching sight of another tabloid in the kitchen wastebasket.

He was leaning against the counter, his suit jacket and tie discarded, his shirt sleeves rolled up. He'd set the table and cut the bread, and now he was watching as she prepared dinner.

Natalie had always been a health-conscious cook, but now that Mick was on his nutritional kick and was handing out recipes to anyone who would listen, she'd taken advantage of his expertise and had streamlined her cooking methods even more.

"I don't."

"Then why did you buy it?"

"Because I think there's someone out to get me."

"Baby, you're getting paranoid."

"I don't think so."

"Who do you think it is?"

"Michelle. She's never forgiven Maurice for what he did to her, giving me that dress. I'm not stupid, Luke—"

"I never said you were."

"I hear what's being said about me and I don't like it! She hasn't been working as much as she usually does, so perhaps she's supplementing her income by selling her speculations about us to the *National Star!*"

His hand settled on her tight shoulder, gently massaging the tense muscles. "Forget about it. Most of it's innuendo, none of it has any substance—"

"I thought you didn't read the tabloids!"

"I have someone who does. The minute they overstep their bounds, I'll have my lawyer call."

He did such an effortless job of protecting her. She spooned the shrimp stir-fry dish out of the wok and on to two plates, turned off the burner, then set down the pan and went into his arms.

"I'm sorry." They'd been apart for almost a week. She'd been on a shoot in Palm Beach, he'd been in the midst of closing another deal. It was their first evening home together, and she was wasting time with a silly argument.

"I'm sorry, too."

"I don't want to fight with you."

"That was a fight?" He kissed her, then picked up their plates and carried them to the small, round table in the corner of the large kitchen.

"I *try* not to fight with you," she amended, smiling as she got out a bottle of wine and swiftly opened it. "You're too good a negotiator."

They talked of other things, but over dessert, Luke surprised her.

"You really have a feeling that this Michelle is bad-mouthing you?"

"I do."

"I'll see what I can do."

The sense of calm that settled over her was overwhelming. She felt safe with Luke. Protected. Her career was important to her, but none of it would have mattered without this man in her life.

Though he'd been honest with her from the start, and told her he would never marry again and had no desire to have a family, she considered them to be a family.

The two of them against the world.

SOMETHING WAS VERY WRONG.

Natalie sensed it, could almost feel it. She'd asked Monique to meet her for lunch, and now watched as the elegant blond Frenchwoman made her way through the fashionable luncheon crowd at one of New York's hottest new restaurants.

The food was Italian, and reputed to be superb. Mick and his wife had eaten here the weekend before, and he'd recommended it to her. Natalie had asked for a table in one of the shadowy corners. She wanted some privacy for what she had to say.

She waited until they were into their first course before bringing up her fears. She trusted Monique and knew the woman would give her a straight answer if she had any information.

"I feel like things are slipping with my career," she said finally, willing the nerves in her stomach to settle down.

"I know what you mean," Monique replied levelly.

The sense of relief that washed over Natalie calmed her. Monique might be considered many things, but she was honest to a fault. She'd never lied to Natalie in the course of their relationship, and now, with the older woman's response to what she'd said, Natalie knew her fears had some justification.

"Do you know what's going on?" she asked Monique.

"No. But I can make some discreet inquiries to a few old friends." Most of Monique's business acquaintances were also friends. It was just her way. Especially since her husband had died, Monique had made the business, and the people in that business, part of her family.

"In the meantime," she said softly, "say nothing about this to anyone."

"I've already told Luke—"

"Of course you've told him. The two of you are like two halves of a whole. But no one else, do you understand? We must take care of this problem immediately."

"Would you have done something if I hadn't talked to you about it?" Natalie asked.

For the first time in her life, she saw Monique Devereux look worried. Only an instant, but it had been there, in her eyes.

"I'm already looking for the one who I believe has betrayed you," she said, her voice without expression. "But whoever it is, they're covering their tracks well."

WITHIN TWO WEEKS, they knew who it was.

Natalie glanced up from beneath a stylist's ministrations to see Luke standing in front of her.

"Come with me. Quickly."

She didn't think to disobey him. The stylist stared, openmouthed, as Luke put his arm around her and hustled her out of the studio.

"Luke, I—"

"No time. Get in the car."

The limousine was waiting, parked in an alley behind the building. As she slipped inside, she could hear noise and commotion in the streets in front of the studio.

"Let's go," Luke said quietly to his driver. The long black car started with a muffled purr and slid out the back way and into the anonymity of New York traffic.

"What happened?" she asked, her voice tight.

He was looking out the tinted window at nothing. The muscles in his jaw were tight, almost rigid. She sensed he was fighting to keep his considerable temper in check.

"Luke?"

He turned then, all aggression going out of his body as he enfolded her in his arms.

"We've got to get you home before they get there."

She closed her eyes and leaned her cheek against his chest. Her world was rapidly spinning out of control, and Luke was the only solid part of it. She trusted him with her heart and her life, and she would trust him now.

They reached the Garner Building in record time, and before she had time to collect her thoughts, they were upstairs in the penthouse they'd shared for the past two years. Safely at home.

She sat on the couch in his office and watched him as he talked on the phone. First, he canceled all his appointments. Then he called Monique, then Mick, and finally Maurice Kouris in Paris.

Monique arrived within the hour, Mick minutes later. The four of them sat in the large conference room two floors below the apartments and tried to decide what was to be done.

An influential friend of Luke's had phoned him with the news that a special edition of the *National Star* was going to come out that evening, and that the stories inside could potentially damage Natalie's career. But he hadn't been able to find out the exact content.

Luke had gone directly to Natalie, not wanting her to be deluged by reporters eager to witness her first reaction to the news.

Now, they had to find out what was being printed, see how much damage had been done and figure out how it could be contained.

"The issue will be out this evening," Mick confirmed. "My wife is at one of the first newsstands that gets a delivery, and she's promised to buy one and come right up."

"I'll send a car for her," Luke said quietly.

They waited around the conference table, and while it couldn't have been more than an hour and a half, it seemed like a lifetime to Natalie.

When Gina, Mick's wife, finally entered the room, the tension in the air was palpable. She walked straight to Natalie, handed her the tabloid, then patted her shoulder awkwardly.

"I'm so sorry," she whispered, then turned toward Mick and took his hand.

Within seconds after she read the various sensational headlines on the front of the tabloid, Natalie felt herself going into shock. She had to force herself to turn the pages, force herself to read what had been written about the most private moments of her life.

Only three people knew about what had been sensationalized within the pages of this paper.

Mick, Jane and Marta.

Four, if you counted Luke, but she didn't.

Natalie looked up at Mick, absolute rage on her face.

He seemed genuinely puzzled, and she swallowed her anger, not wanting to believe it could be him. She barely felt Luke come to stand behind her, barely registered the feel of his hands on her shoulders, offering wordless comfort and support.

She simply turned the pages, wondering what kind of person could even think of invading someone's personal life to such an extent. And how they could have thought of going public with it.

She was halfway through the tabloid when a picture caught her attention and everything within her went perfectly still. Natalie remembered pictures, remembered when they were taken, the mood behind them, even more than the finished photos themselves.

In this particular picture, she was sitting beneath a palm tree on the beach, waving at the photographer.

The Palm Beach shoot.

Late afternoon.

They'd all gone out dancing afterward.

The photograph had been taken at the end of the day, toward the end of the light, just before they'd all gone to the hotel to clean up.

It had been taken with a pocket-size camera, by someone who didn't shoot photographs for a living.

She glanced at the people around her. Monique, concern etching her patrician features. Mick, a certain sense of despair in his expression. Gina, his wife, tears in her eyes. Gina had had time to skim most of the tabloid articles during the ride over. And being from a large Italian family, she certainly understood how painful it felt to have your family attacked.

And Luke. She felt his presence behind her, and needed his strength desperately. Her world had fallen apart, and she had no idea how she was going to go on in the face of such a massive betrayal.

She reached for his hand, and he gave it to her, his fingers warm and strong as they curled around hers and held them tightly. Natalie wet her dry lips and tried to take a breath into her tight chest. She swallowed, hoping she could get the words out before breaking down completely.

"It was Marta."

A SHORT TIME LATER, she left the conference room for the bedroom she shared with Luke, and refused even his company. She didn't want to break down in front of any of them. The absolute despair she felt was too great.

She'd been nine when her father left, almost ten when her grandmother had died. The woman had embodied all the strength and wisdom their family possessed, and Natalie's mother, though she was beautiful and loved her daughter with everything she had, simply hadn't been strong enough.

Her third breakdown had resulted in her hospitalization, and Natalie had been sent to her first foster home.

She'd told Mick the story one night, over drinks, after a particularly rigorous shoot. He'd listened carefully and comforted her when she'd confided her greatest fear, that someday she was going to share the same destiny as her mother.

"It's normal to feel pressure in this business," he'd said. "I think you would have broken by now. You're strong, Natalie. You'll survive."

She'd been working with Jane and Marta in London the night Jane had broken things off with her boyfriend. They'd been engaged, and the English model had been devastated. Natalie had listened to her, far into the night, even up to the point where Jane, sobbing, confessed she thought she was going to lose her mind.

They'd talked through the entire night, and Natalie had told her about her mother, about the fear and rage and helplessness she'd felt. About how completely alone in the world she'd been. No one had understood. No one could. She'd been made to feel ashamed of her mother's weakness, her inability to care for her daughter.

She'd told Jane about her mother as a means of expressing her empathy for what her friend was feeling. It had worked. By the time the sun had come up over London's rooftops, Jane had felt as if she was able to go on.

Marta had awakened during the night, come into the bedroom, sat on the bed and listened quietly. And

Natalie had been so concerned for Jane that she hadn't given a thought to the other woman.

Besides, she'd thought Marta was her friend. Marta had been the quietest of the three, and Natalie and Jane had spent considerable time building up Marta's self-confidence. When she'd come down with pneumonia, both of them had visited her steadily through the long illness, neither of them drifting away as Marta's illness stretched from weeks to months.

Natalie had even tried to help her get several choice modeling assignments once she'd returned to work.

Now, Marta was telling the world that Natalie was basically unstable. During the six weeks Natalie had spent with Luke in Aruba, Marta—a very close and concerned friend—claimed she'd been in a private psychiatric hospital Luke had found for her. She'd been hidden away, suffering from her first nervous breakdown.

Just like her mother.

Marta had also claimed that Natalie's mental health was the reason for her relationship with Luke in the first place. She'd given Luke complete control of her body, any sexual favor he desired, in trade for the guarantee that Luke would use his money and power to take care of her, insure her the finest medical care, while she suffered these breakdowns.

After all, the article claimed, it was only a matter of time...

The most painful insinuation had been that the state of her mental health was the reason Luke hadn't married her.

The entire nightmare was beyond comprehension. Beyond bearing. She lay down on the bed and pulled the covers over her head.

The assignments she hadn't been selected for, the various shoots that other models had been given. The oversights by major cosmetics companies, the feeling she'd had that her career was slowly slipping. Everything began to make a horrible sort of sense.

The pitying looks she'd sensed from several makeup artists and stylists. The whispers among other models that had pointedly stopped when she'd entered a room.

Perfect, horrible sense.

Natalie finally broke.

She cried until she couldn't cry anymore, for herself and her mother. For the fact that something so very private and painful had been twisted, perverted, used against her.

She had no idea how much time had passed before she heard the soft knock at the door. She didn't answer. Couldn't. She turned her face away from the door, then heard it open and close gently.

Luke.

He didn't say a word, simply sat down on the bed, then lay down next to her and took her in his arms.

She couldn't seem to stop crying.

There were no words to explain how deeply this had hurt, and he didn't offer any. He held her as she cried, then handed her tissues as he stayed close to her side.

"I have Maurice on the phone in the conference room," he said. "He wants to talk to you."

"It doesn't make any difference."

"Why?"

"I'm never going to work again."

"Nat, I don't think that—"

"No. I don't want to be a part of it."

He was silent for several minutes, holding her.

"So you're going to drop out. Just like that?"

"Just like that."

"Then she gets exactly what she wants."

"I don't give a damn what that bitch gets or wants."

"Don't do this, Natalie—"

"She was my mother, Luke. My *mother.*"

He held her tightly for a few more minutes, then gently pulled her to her feet.

"Maurice is a good man, and he's been good to you. At least come down and say hello."

She knew what he was trying to do, and she also knew she couldn't hide in their bedroom for the rest of her life.

"All right. But I'm going to tell him I'm quitting."

"Whatever you want, baby."

Monique was talking on the phone with Maurice when they entered the conference room. She was speaking rapidly in French, her tone low, her manner urgent. She quickly wound up the conversation as Natalie approached her.

"Talk to Maurice," she urged. "Luke is right, the damage is already done. Now we must fight to contain it."

Natalie took the phone and sat down at the large conference table.

"Hello."

"Natalie. I'm sorry to hear what has happened."

"Me, too."

"She'll never work for me again."

"Thank you."

"Now, what do you plan to do?"

"Nothing."

A short silence ensued as Maurice took this in.

"Nothing?"

"Yes."

"Maybe, for now, the way you feel, it is a good idea."

"No. I mean nothing ever again."

"Natalie. Did you think this was never going to happen?"

She felt Luke's hand on her shoulder and covered it with her own.

"Did Monique tell you what happened?"

"Some of it. Gina told me what was in the paper."

"So you understand."

"I understand how you feel. But not why you would want to quit."

"I've made enough money—"

"It's not about money. Let me ask you this, why do you think she did it?"

"I don't really care."

"She's scared. Of you. You have it all, darling. Qualities she will never have. Marta knows you have what it takes to succeed, all the way to the very top."

"But I don't want it anymore."

"It happened with me, as well. The rumors. First, that I liked little girls. Then, that I liked alcohol so much I couldn't be trusted to design and mount a show."

"Who did it?" She was interested in his story in spite of herself.

"A friend. I thought she was a friend. I'd hoped we could mean something more to each other."

"How did you—" She lowered her voice. "How did you go on?"

"I thought of revenge. Daily." He laughed, a deep, rumbling sound. "Hourly. That wasted almost six months of my life. Then, my fingers started to itch for a pencil, and I began to draw again. You love what you do, Natalie, and you'll come back to it."

"I've thought about leaving before this."

"You'll leave when you discover what it is you want to do next. Until then, come work for me. Spend a few months in Europe until this whole ugly incident blows over, eh?"

"You think it will?"

"It will if you don't call attention to yourself by doing exactly what she wants you to do."

That silenced her.

"Luke will try to get his revenge, but you must not let him. I would do the same for my wife, so I understand his impulse to protect you. Don't let him do it. Don't call attention to her, don't give her any more help."

She didn't say anything, and Maurice continued, his voice low and urgent.

"Marta was a good, solid model, but nothing special. She wasn't you, Natalie. If you're smart, and let this entire thing die down, so will her career. She doesn't have what you have. But let that happen by itself."

"Yes." She could feel the tension in her muscles leaving, could feel Luke's gentle squeeze of reassurance.

"Come to Europe. Between myself and my friends, we'll have enough work for you to prove to the world you're a reliable woman."

"Maurice—" Tears were filling her eyes, choking her throat.

"You were stunning in my little black dress. The hit of the show, *minou*. Remember?"

She nodded, overcome with emotion.

"Don't let her finish you, Natalie."

"Okay." The one word hurt her throat, but she knew Maurice was well aware of what he'd done and how much it meant to her.

She hung up the phone and took Luke's hand firmly in her own. He was smiling at her, and she had a feeling he knew what she was going to say.

"I'm going to Europe to work for Maurice."

LUKE MOVED HIS BASE of operations to Paris, and the time they spent there proved to be some of the happiest months Natalie could remember.

She threw herself into work with a vengeance, maintaining such long hours that often she'd come home to their Paris apartment and go straight to bed. Luke never criticized her. He seemed happy to see her working again.

Natalie knew that the photographs would make their way across the Atlantic, and that people in the business would know she hadn't rolled over and died.

Then Luke surprised her again.

"I'm having dinner with a director Tuesday night," he said, naming a well-known multiple Oscar winner. "He'd like to meet you."

Since she loved the director's films, she agreed to come along.

It was a fascinating night, the upshot of which was that the director wanted Natalie to take a small part in his latest film.

"I've never acted before," she said, trying to hide the fact that the idea was intriguing to her.

"The camera loves your face. It's a small part, and I'd coach you through it."

Filming began in New York in three months, and before dinner was over, she'd agreed to do it.

Natalie knew acting was deceptively hard work. Before the project began, she read several books and managed to squeeze in a few classes with a respected teacher without the director's knowledge. As nervous as she was when shooting began, the entire experience was an exhilarating one.

She found she liked being pushed to her limits. It was so different from modeling, with very specific skills being called into play. When filming was finally over, she flew back to Paris, and Luke. She'd have to come back and do some post-production work, but that was several weeks away.

Then Maurice surprised her one more time.

"It's the right time for you to go back, but we need something to showcase your return," he said one evening. The fashion designer had invited Luke and Natalie to his château outside Paris for the weekend, and they were sitting outside, drinking wine.

"Do you have any ideas?" Luke asked. She could tell that he was interested in Maurice's idea. He'd been discussing something along the same lines with her, and she was glad both men agreed on this particular piece of timing.

"A book of photos. Beautifully done. Some nudity, but nothing in bad taste. Coffee-table size. The photos would be done by people I trust, and I would write the introduction. As a lover of beauty, of course."

Luke glanced at her. She could tell he was fired up by the idea, but wanted to hear her opinion first.

"All right," she said. She'd missed New York and Denver, missed working at home. She'd been in Europe almost ten months.

"I'll talk to some people I know in publishing," Luke said. "It's a good idea, Maurice."

Looking at her lover across the table, Natalie knew Luke would make the book of photos a *New York Times* best-seller if he had to call in every single favor he'd ever been owed.

"To success," Maurice said, lifting his wineglass in a toast. Natalie raised hers, then reached for Luke's hand across the table. Their eyes met, and she saw admiration in his. And all at once she was glad she hadn't given up on her career.

Once again, the possibilities seemed limitless.

"To success," she said, then leaned across the table and kissed Luke.

It was time to go home.

Chapter Nine

She started spotting on their fourth day in Fairplay.

Luke had gone out with Otis to replenish the woodpile, and she was alone in the kitchen of the cabin when she felt the warm, sticky dampness between her legs.

Once in the bathroom, she had to emotionally confront what that blood meant.

Trying to keep her escalating emotions under control, she called Doc. He came directly to the cabin and checked her. Then he helped her into bed, tucking the covers around her and plumping the down pillows.

"It's not a good sign, Natalie," he said, honest to a fault. She was grateful for that, at least. Grateful for his honesty and the compassion she saw in his bright blue eyes.

He'd been holding her hand, and she squeezed it. "Maybe it's best that I never told him," she whispered, hating even to think about what might be happening inside her body.

"Now, that's not what I meant," Doc said gruffly. He'd been sitting on the chair next to the bed, and he moved so he was sitting on the bed looking at her.

"I've known women who spotted throughout their entire pregnancies and delivered healthy babies. So I don't want you believing that this little one is leaving us just yet."

She smiled shakily, then dissolved into tears. It was so frustrating, being pregnant. It seemed that all she ever did was sleep, have morning sickness or cry. And though Doc was a great comfort to her, she wanted Luke.

He'd always been her champion. Any sort of emergency or disaster seemed to bring out the best in him. Now, in the middle of one of the most emotional moments of her entire life, she wished he was here with Doc. Luke had a way of making her feel safe.

"Now, that's all right, you just let it out. It can't have been very pleasant, these last few days, what with the secret you've been keeping."

"I want him to want the baby."

"I know you do."

"I don't want him to leave me."

"I know."

Then she heard the front door slam and the sound of booted feet running up the stairs. Luke burst into the bedroom, his gaze going first to her, then Doc. He was at her side in an instant, looking down at her. She saw fear in his eyes.

"I saw Doc's car. What the hell's going on?"

She burst into tears and he took her into his arms and rocked her. Natalie closed her eyes, feeling like a total mess.

All her life, she'd yearned for a family. She could remember how it had felt when they'd taken her mother away to the psychiatric ward as if it had happened only the day before. Now she was afraid the child she carried would cause Luke to leave her, and she didn't think she was strong enough to contemplate a life without him.

Doc was packing his black bag and was about to leave the bedroom when Luke waylaid him.

"Doc, wait a minute. Tell me what's going on."

And Natalie held her breath, wondering if Doc would keep his promise.

Kindly blue eyes gazed at her intently, as if to say, *Now's the perfect time.* When fear kept her silent, the old man sighed and turned to Luke.

"I want her to stay in bed for the remainder of the day. She's exhausted and needs to rest."

"We shouldn't have walked to the café—"

"I don't want you blaming yourself, son. These things just happen. Now, what she needs is rest and a little love, and I think you're just the man to give her what she needs."

Luke nodded, and Natalie could sense the emotion he was keeping tightly under control.

"And Natalie," Doc continued, "don't let your emotions get the better of you." He leaned over the bed and smoothed her hair off her forehead. "Nothing's going to go wrong. You've got your young man with you, and you know I'm here if you need me. I'll tell Mae to send over some food for the two of you, but you've got to relax and let yourself rest."

She nodded, all the while feeling that things were fast escalating out of control.

LUKE WOULD HAVE STAYED upstairs with her, but Doc motioned for him to come downstairs.

"She's a high-strung little thing," he muttered as he reached the front door of the cabin.

"She is," Luke agreed.

"Sometimes a woman can create her own problems, if you know what I mean."

"I do."

He walked Doc out to his car, a bright red Jeep. Doc placed his black bag on the passenger seat, slammed the door shut, then turned toward Luke.

"Do you mind if I ask a personal question?"

"No."

"Why haven't you married that little girl?"

Luke smiled at the old man's quiet outrage. It seemed that everyone in Fairplay championed Natalie, whether she was aware of it or not.

"I've got a ring on its way, and I'm asking her tomorrow night. It's our four-year anniversary."

Doc studied him for a long moment, and he wondered what the older man was thinking.

"What time will this ring arrive?"

"It should be here by three."

"Don't wait. Ask her today."

He had that strange feeling that something was going on beneath the surface that he couldn't quite get a handle on.

"What's going on, Doc?"

"I made a promise to that girl upstairs, and I can't bring myself to break it. But I'll tell you this. If you propose to her tonight and you find out what's bothering her, you come talk to me. I don't care what time it is. I'm here for you, too, Luke."

He watched Doc walk around to the driver's side of the Jeep and climb inside. Luke was just about to go inside when Doc honked the horn.

When he reached the driver's side window, Doc gave him a sharp look.

"I don't like meddling in a man's personal affairs, if you know what I mean."

"I understand."

"If you should need me, I'll be at the medical center over in Breckenridge most of Saturday afternoon and into the night. I was hoping to make the dance, but I'm not sure I'll be home in time."

"Should I still ask her if she wants to go, or would it be too much for her?"

"I'd let her go, if she feels up to it. Don't let her sit alone in that room and get too broody, son. Keep an eye on her."

"I will. Thanks, Doc."

The older man nodded, and for a moment Luke sensed his tiredness. Doc certainly loved his work, caring for his mountain people, but there had to be moments when he became frustrated.

He watched as Doc drove away, and his natural impatience asserted itself as he thought about going inside and asking Natalie to simply tell him what was the matter. But he didn't want to cause her any more stress, and the engagement ring he'd requested would be here by late afternoon. So he'd wait until it arrived, and then ask her to marry him.

OTIS WAS out by the woodpile, still stacking the cords of wood. Luke caught the worried expression on his face and reassured him immediately.

"She's all right. She called Doc because she didn't feel good, and he came right over. She's sleeping now, but I'm going to keep an eye on her for the rest of the day."

"We won't expect you at the poker game tonight, then. Unless," Otis said, scratching his chin thoughtfully, "unless you'd like to play poker over here tonight."

Luke knew that Natalie would probably sleep most of the evening away. And he also knew that he needed something, anything, to serve as a distraction from his problems. Maybe if he concentrated on a game of cards, it would rest his brain enough so that the answer to this whole puzzle would come clear.

"I'd appreciate it."

"Then don't you worry about a thing. Me and the boys'll stop by the Nugget and get some food, and we'll have ourselves a good time."

THE RING ARRIVED a little after three in the afternoon, via private messenger. Luke paid the man, then walked onto the porch and opened the small, black velvet box.

The stone was exquisite, a two-carat diamond surrounded by sapphires and set in platinum. Though Natalie wasn't the sort of woman who worshiped jewelry, he knew she would cherish this ring for what it represented far more than for the value of the stones.

He tucked the box in his shirt front and, his heart pounding, started up the stairs.

It didn't matter that he'd known her almost four years and lived with her most of that time. It didn't matter that they had been as intimate as two people could be. He was still asking her to marry him, and for Luke, that was an enormous step.

His first, and only, attempt at marriage had ended disastrously. He'd berated himself mercilessly for the fact that he hadn't been smart enough to see through to his ex-wife's true nature.

She'd been a cunning woman and played him for a total sap. By the time the terms of their divorce had been hammered out, he'd felt as if she'd simply driven an armored car up to his bank account and emptied it.

His money had been the main attraction, after all.

Luke knew he'd been cautious after that, never letting himself get too attached to any one woman. He'd dated an entire group of females at a time, enjoying himself enormously. He had a healthy sexuality and had played the field with a vengeance.

But something had always been missing, though he'd pushed his feelings away and tried not to think too hard about what it was he really wanted.

Then he'd seen her picture.

His first impulse had been to possess her. Wine and dine her, impress the hell out of her and get her into bed with him in record time.

But Natalie had been a total surprise.

He'd loved her from the start, if he'd been honest with himself. By the time that first dance had been over, he'd fallen hard and had fought that emotion by making sure he kept everything under his control.

Where they went. What they did. How often they saw each other. He'd been patient, but all the time the plan had been to bind her to him so tightly that she'd never want to run away.

She'd run twice, once when she'd come up to this town in the mountains to build her cabin, once just days ago. She didn't run without a reason. The first time she'd come to Fairplay, she'd been fighting private demons from the past. Now, he didn't know what they were up against.

He reached the top of the stairs and stood outside the bedroom door.

She'd wanted marriage. He would have to have been a total fool not to have seen that. Natalie was the sort of woman who would only bloom with a husband and children at her side. There had been times when he'd known, deep in his soul, that he was a selfish man keeping her as his companion. His lover.

His mistress.

He could rationalize all he wanted, but deep inside he knew that a good marriage changed a relationship, and for the better. Made it more solid. Promised a future. As Luke stared at the door and thought about what he was going to ask Natalie, he wondered why he hadn't done it long ago.

Hell, he loved her so much he'd even consider having a child.

Before, he'd never wanted any woman to have that kind of an emotional hold over him. His ex had wanted to get pregnant, but as a method of manipulation. Once she'd been firmly burrowed in as the mother of his child, nothing could have dislodged her.

Natalie was completely different. She would never play the same sort of emotional games with him. In the years they'd been together, he'd never known her to be deliberately cruel.

She'd make a wonderful wife and a giving, loving mother.

Luke fingered the ring box in his pocket, wondering what had happened to frighten Natalie. And he wondered why she didn't trust him enough to tell him what was really going on.

He'd never loved anyone the way he loved Natalie. He'd gladly spend the rest of his life fighting all her dragons, making sure she was safe, keeping every dream she ever had close to his heart.

Opening the door silently, he slipped inside the bedroom. She was still asleep, but he wouldn't wake her. Settling himself in the chair next to the bed, he carefully swung his legs onto the foot of the bed and settled down to wait.

He'd been patient for a long time, and he could wait a little longer.

WHEN SHE WOKE UP, he was sitting by her side.

"Hi," she said self-consciously, pushing her hair out of her eyes.

"How're you feeling?"

"Better."

Looking at Luke, she knew the time had come to tell him the truth. She could tell he was nervous, especially since Doc's visit. It wasn't fair to keep him in ignorance of everything that had happened. She was still scared he might leave her, but she hated knowing that she was the source of his worries.

Above all, she loved him and wanted him to know what had happened between them. What they had created.

And if she was totally honest with herself, she was no longer sure how he was going to react.

"Luke, there's something I have to tell you."

He smiled, a smile so full of love she felt warmed inside.

"There's something I have to ask you."

Does he know? Has he guessed? Has Doc told him?

Luke didn't seem upset. Encouraged by this, she patted the bed and moved over so he could sit next to her. She sensed he was nervous, and wondered why. Looking into his face, with her heart in her eyes, she smiled encouragingly.

"Natalie," he said, taking her hand, "will you marry me?"

IT WAS THE LAST THING she'd thought he would say.

"Oh, no!" The words burst out of her mouth before she thought of how he might react. The absolute and complete shock she felt must have shown in her face, because he frowned.

Her mind was racing furiously. How could she possibly agree to marry him when he didn't know she was pregnant? How could they begin a marriage with a deception that crucial? She had to find a way to select the correct words, she had to stay calm.

She'd always known Luke possessed a quick, fiery, emotional temper, but she'd never known him to direct it at her. Now, feeling his anger and frustration, she realized she'd made a terrible mistake in not trusting to fate and giving him an immediate yes.

Because Luke was a man who needed to know she believed in him.

He'd always been totally loyal to her, he'd fought her battles and believed in her completely. And he expected the same in return.

The longer the silence stretched, the worse it became.

"Luke, I—"

"It's all right."

With sudden insight she realized that though Luke was a businessman extraordinaire and had made millions of dollars and deals, when it came to matters of the heart he was simply a man.

A man who, at this moment, believed she didn't want him.

"It's not what you think—"

"Then tell me what it is." His voice was too quiet, and she knew she'd hurt him deeply.

Emotion overwhelmed her. Why had their timing been so very wrong? He'd finally decided marriage was something he wanted. She'd never nagged him about making that particular commitment, but she hadn't denied she wanted to marry him.

Yet now she had to tell him that on the brink of getting used to thinking of himself as a husband, he was going to become a father.

Even though she usually behaved like a rational human being, and even though Doc had told her that her pregnancy was no one's fault, feelings of guilt overwhelmed her.

Luke stood up slowly and headed toward the door. And Natalie knew, with utmost emotional certainty, that her time had finally run out.

HE COULDN'T KEEP his mind on the game.

Otis had brought Sam and Pete over, along with enough barbecued ribs, baked beans, corn and cole-slaw to feed an army. Baking powder biscuits and two cherry cobblers completed the dinner, but Luke didn't do justice to any of it.

More than anything, he listened. And thought of Natalie, upstairs in their bed.

And wondered what the hell he was going to do with the rest of his life.

The three men were good company. He tried to focus his attention on them as they started the weekly poker game. Luke learned that Pete and Sam had last names, Harris and Russell. And that, while Otis had been a cowboy, Pete had been a wrangler and worked with horses, while Sam had worked in construction.

And all of them were bored silly by retirement.

"Doc had the right idea," said Pete as he expertly dealt the cards. "Got into something he can do until he dies."

"And it's pretty damn interesting, doctorin' the people up here," Sam remarked, picking up his cards and considering them.

"You gonna tell us what's bothering you?" Otis asked Luke as he picked up his last card. "As if I didn't already know." He glanced at the ceiling, toward the master bedroom.

"I'd rather not talk about it," Luke said quietly.

"Hell, we're all men at this table," Pete said conversationally. "None of us understand women any more than you do. Now, what's got that little beauty all upset, and why are you twisting those cards around in your hand?"

"I just don't understand what the hell she wants!"

"You said it, brother," Sam mumbled.

"Probably wants to get married," Otis said, considering his hand. "They all do, sooner or later."

"Not so bad, being caught," said Pete. "Long as she lets you think you're still in charge."

Luke hadn't planned on telling them that he'd proposed that afternoon, but the entire story came tumbling out.

"You know a hell of a lot about business, my boy," said Pete, picking up a card and discarding another. "But you know nothing about the way to a woman's heart."

Luke bristled. "And what's that?"

"Flowers," said Sam.

"Romance," said Otis.

"Walks on a moonlit beach," said Pete. "Kind of hard to do here in Fairplay, I'll grant you that. But we get by with the Platte River. Looks kind of pretty at night."

"I wouldn't have chosen this time or place to propose to Natalie," Luke said evenly, trying to keep his temper in check. "But when I told Doc I was going to ask Natalie to marry me, he suggested I do it as soon as possible."

The three men digested this fact.

"Maybe she's pregnant," Otis finally remarked.

"Impossible."

"Is she mean and ornery?" Sam asked.

"Sick in the mornings?" Pete added.

"Cries all the time, at the drop of a hat?" Otis chimed in.

"Natalie's never mean, but she has been acting kind of strange." Luke thought back to the morning she'd locked him out of the bathroom. "And she's been sick. And all she does is cry."

"Pregnant," said Sam.

"Yep," said Pete.

"She sure is," added Otis.

Luke felt a peculiar kind of roaring in his ears, and a part of him realized he was going into shock.

"Now, let me ask you this," Pete continued, taking another card from the deck and discarding one of the ones in his hand. "How do you think she thinks you're going to react?"

It took him a moment to collect his thoughts.

Natalie, pregnant? With his child? Luke knew birth control could fail, and he also knew with absolute certainty that this pregnancy had been an accident. And knowing Natalie, she'd still be feeling guilty.

The dinner. She'd been planning to tell him that night. He hadn't come home in time, and she'd retreated to her cabin to figure out what to do.

And he, in true heroic fashion, had raced after her and not given her a moment's peace.

Talk about guilt.

"What?" he asked, glancing at Pete.

"How do you think she thinks you're going to react?"

He thought of all the times he'd assured her he wasn't the type of man who wanted to be married or have a family. And slowly his anger at her dissipated, to be replaced with empathy.

He knew Natalie. She had a strong sense of honor, and wouldn't have wanted to do anything that would seem as if she was trying to trap him.

And an unplanned pregnancy would have made it impossible for her to accept his proposal of marriage, no matter how much she might love him.

She's still trying to get up the nerve to tell me.

It was why she'd asked him to stay with her for a week. She'd needed a little time. They were complete opposites. He was full of impatience and wanted to close a deal, while she liked to carefully consider all the angles and do what was best for all concerned.

Suddenly, everything fell into place, and he had all the information he needed. Luke felt he was in control again.

"Well," said Pete. "What do you think she thinks?"

"I don't think she'd believe I'd be happy about it."

"Then that's what all the crazy behavior has been about," Sam declared. "Now that this particular problem has been solved, gentlemen, can we get back to playing cards?"

"I should tell her I know," Luke said quietly.

"Give it some time," Pete advised.

"Let her come to you," Otis advised.

"Pick up a card!" Sam said, glaring at Pete.

The expectant father played poker in a daze, trying to control the various emotions flooding over him. He'd never thought about even attempting to become a father until today, right before he proposed to Natalie. To know that he was already in that position was overwhelming.

"Hang on, I'll be right back," he said, then put his cards facedown on the kitchen table and headed toward the stairs.

"Glad to be of service," Pete called after him.

SHE WAS FAST ASLEEP.

He was reminded of the day he'd walked into the bedroom, only three days ago. She looked peaceful from a distance, but when he took a closer look at her face, it was red and blotchy from crying.

She must have been terrified.

He forgave her in that instant. He'd never been able to stay mad at Natalie. She might do some pretty emotional things, she might act impulsively without thinking things through, but she had a good heart and had never acted out of malice. And she'd never tried to manipulate him.

He went downstairs and enjoyed several hours of poker. He and Pete ended up winning the most money, and Luke promised to buy them all drinks at the J Bar J the following night at the dance.

"Bring the little mother," Pete added as Luke walked the three men to the front door.

"Listen," Luke said as he followed them onto the porch. "Don't say anything to anyone about Natalie's condition just yet. Can I trust the three of you?"

"Tell Mae?" Otis snorted. "Might as well tell the entire town, and put it on the front page of the *Denver Post* to boot."

"I can keep a secret," Sam promised.

"Count me in," said Pete.

"I won't say a thing," Otis replied.

Luke cleared his throat. "I appreciate what the three of you did for me tonight. You saved me a hell of a lot of worrying."

"Men have to stick together," Pete muttered. "Women are downright scary when you think about it."

"Yeah," Luke said, grinning. "I know exactly what you mean."

HE TOOK OFF HIS CLOTHES and slid into bed with her, and she woke as she felt his arms come around her.

"Luke?" she whispered.

"I'm so sorry, baby."

This time, when she cried, he understood why. He stroked her hair, her back, all the while murmuring soothing, comforting words.

"I didn't mean to hurt you."

"I know. It's all right. Don't get upset, remember what Doc said—"

"I know, but—"

"Shh."

When she finally calmed down, he got out of bed and found the little black box, then brought it to her. Without saying a word, he took the ring out of the jeweler's box and slipped it on her finger.

"Just try to get rid of me, Nat," he teased, and was rewarded by a tired, relieved smile.

"I wanted to say yes," she whispered.

"I know."

"Please don't leave me, Luke."

He knew what she was really saying, and held her tightly.

"I'm not going anywhere."

He'd left the bedside lamp on, and studied her body covertly. He'd missed the subtle fullness of her breasts. She'd always had generous curves, but now there was a new ripeness to her body, a lushness. He was surprised at the emotional impulses that came to life deep inside him, to protect her, to watch over her. To make sure nothing happened to her while she was carrying their child.

More than anything, he wished she would tell him.

Trust me, Natalie, Luke thought as she drifted off to sleep in his arms.

He knew everything that frightened her because he'd gotten to know her nightmares well over the years. He knew she still missed her mother.

He knew how much this baby had already come to mean to Natalie. And how emotionally perilous the journey to motherhood would be for her. She hadn't had a mother of her own for a long time.

And he knew, with a deep contentment he'd never before experienced, that he wanted to be right by her side, close to her heart, every single step of the way.

Chapter Ten

The book of photos, titled *Natalie,* was a monstrous success.

It helped that each of Maurice's photographer friends had a different vision of what a beautiful woman was. In their deft, artistic hands, she was transformed from one page to the next, from an innocent, virginal girl to the darkest erotic dream a man could desire.

Natalie climbed up the bestseller lists until it reached the number three spot, where it held steady for sixteen weeks.

"Not bad, your first time out," Luke had teased her.

But it served its purpose, and brought her into the public eye in America with a vengeance.

The work in Europe had helped her. She'd developed a certain career confidence. The time away from familiar places and people had allowed her to get a sense of distance concerning modeling, and now when she went on a shoot, she enjoyed it in a way she never had before.

And it showed.

"These new photographs are gorgeous," Monique remarked quietly. She and Natalie had finished having dinner at her apartment, and now, over coffee, were examining a new set of pictures for her modeling portfolio. "Mick has surpassed himself."

This kind of praise from Monique was rare, and Natalie smiled. She'd been pleased with the results, and was sure the way Mick had photographed her would result in more job offers. She'd come home with an abundance of energy and drive, and having a book on the bestseller list had only piqued the public's interest in her.

She could sell America anything, and the business world knew it.

But she wouldn't have enjoyed any of her success if she hadn't had Luke to share it with. Natalie couldn't understand articles and books she saw about men's fear of women's success. Luke urged her to play longer and harder, to push herself to her absolute limits, to make her career a study in total transcendence.

But, most of all, to be happy.

She'd given him a very personal present while she'd been working on the book. Trusting both Mick and Maurice, she'd had them help her create some extremely erotic shots, for Luke's eyes only.

One night, when he'd arrived home from work, he'd found that she'd placed the photos strategically all over their Paris apartment, along with over fifty votive candles. The highly sexual, visual trail led directly into their bedroom, where she was waiting for him.

He'd told her later he'd never received a better gift.

"You're thinking about him, aren't you?"

Monique's words brought her back to the present. The older woman was eyeing her fondly, the portfolio spread out over her dining room table.

"Yes."

Monique sighed. "Sometimes even these old eyes can be fooled. I didn't think it would last, but it did. You were right, to follow your heart with Luke."

Natalie reached across the table and the short space that separated her from Monique, and took her hand.

"Thank you for not losing faith in me."

Monique gave a particularly Gallic shrug. "I've been in this business since I was fifteen. And I did it all exactly the way I wanted to. No compromises." She lit one of the three Gauloise cigarettes she allowed herself daily and inhaled deeply.

"I promised myself that I would do two things in my career. I wanted to reach the top myself, and I wanted to discover another who would surpass me."

She squeezed Natalie's hand, then let it go and picked up one particular photograph. Mick had caught Natalie looking directly at the camera, a mysterious little half-smile on her face, endless feminine secrets within her eyes.

"And now I have done both."

"WHAT SHALL WE DO with Marta tonight?" Luke called out as he strode into the New York co-op.

"Pull out her fingernails," Natalie answered from the kitchen, where she was making a fresh tomato sauce for pasta.

"Too tame."

"Feed her to the sharks."

"Not torturous enough."

"Make her eat worms."

"You're too nice."

It was a game they played. Natalie had exacted a promise from Luke that he wouldn't go after the woman who had betrayed her, because he'd wanted to destroy Marta completely. Natalie had seen his particular brand of vengeance in action, and realized Luke would never forgive Marta for hurting her.

The understanding that he could finish the woman's career with a few well-placed phone calls to important friends had astounded her. Until she'd become his lover, she'd had no idea what Luke's power entailed.

He teased her as they thought up suitable tortures, but later, after dinner and over coffee, he informed her that Marta had flown to the Coast for a job on a television show.

"Doing what?" Natalie asked.

"Some kind of game show. She's going to give away prizes, that sort of thing."

She couldn't quite bring herself to wish Marta well, but she realized the significance of what this career move meant. Marta was leaving New York and the world of modeling. Her former friend had realized that she'd gone as far as she was going to go, and had left in search of other opportunities.

"How did you find out?" She'd made herself a cappuccino, and Luke an espresso, and they sat by the living room windows, looking out over Central Park and the lights of the city.

"I hired a detective to keep an eye on her a while back."

"When?"

"After she backstabbed you with that tabloid."

She stared at him, astounded.

"You said you didn't want me to hurt her career. You didn't say anything about keeping an eye on her."

"My God, Luke, that's quite an invasion of privacy!"

He took a sip of his espresso, then set the cup down.

"I won't be caught off guard again, Natalie."

She knew she wouldn't win this particular argument. It had been hard enough to make him forfeit the idea of revenge.

"Is this detective still watching her?" she asked.

He simply smiled.

WHEN THEY'D BEEN BACK in the States for five months, he took her to Palm Springs for a vacation. The spa and hotel offered every decadent luxury anyone could want.

Late during the night of their second day there, Luke complained of pains in his chest. When she urged him tō let her take him to the hospital, he refused.

"It's probably something I ate. I'll feel better by morning." He had an early morning tennis game with a business friend, while she was planning to spend her time lying by one of the pools and relaxing in the dry, desert heat.

At four in the morning, she felt his hand, cold and covered with a fine sheen of sweat. He didn't say anything, merely touched her. When she turned on the bedside lamp, she saw he was in such pain he couldn't speak.

She broke every land and speed record getting him to Eisenhower Medical Center.

The emergency room was empty. When the nurse on duty saw Luke's condition, she took him in immediately, leaving Natalie outside with admissions, filling out forms. She had all the information they needed, but her heart was with Luke, beyond the swinging doors and inside the hospital.

Her only comfort was that he was in one of the best medical centers in the country.

"Mrs. Garner?" The woman who had filled out the admitting forms was in her early thirties and had been kind and efficient. "Would you like to go in and see your husband?"

"We're not married," Natalie said quietly.

"Just go on in," the woman replied, obviously trying to comfort her. "Say you're his wife. No one's going to question you."

"Thank you."

She was at Luke's side within minutes. He was lying in a hospital bed, woozy with pain medication. The minute she saw him, her eyes filled with tears.

"I'm fine," he said quietly.

She took his hand, unable to speak, just wanting to touch him and reassure herself that he was still with her.

"Don't cry." The words were soft and slurred, blurred by the pain medication he was being given intravenously.

She shook her head, then pressed her cheek against the back of his hand.

"Sorry...I spoiled...vacation..."

She swallowed her tears as the doctor came in and spoke with her. No, not a heart attack. His heart was in excellent shape. They weren't sure what it was, but it was surely stress-related. Perhaps a change in diet, and several medications to take home...

They had to take him down to the lab for a few X rays, and the doctor gently asked her to wait outside. Natalie walked to the waiting room and sat in one of the chairs closest to the swinging doors, her legs tucked up beneath her. Curled up into a tight ball, she felt less afraid.

She hated hospitals and what they represented. She hated the memories they brought flooding back. But most of all, she hated feeling so very powerless when the person she loved the most on this earth was in such terrible pain.

HER GOALS, HER VERY LIFE, changed soon after that night.

"I'm going to build us a vacation cabin," she told Luke one morning over breakfast at their Denver penthouse.

They had fought over his workload after he'd been discharged from the hospital. He'd resumed a regular schedule despite what the doctor had advised. The only area she could control was his diet, because she still cooked for him almost every night.

Now, she was making plans to help Luke ease himself out of the fast lane.

"What?" He set his paper down, and she knew from the expression on his face that he'd heard what she'd said.

"I'm going to build a cabin. In Fairplay. It should take just a few months if I get enough help."

"Why don't you hire someone else to do it?" he asked. She could tell he was curious as to what was going on with her.

"No. I have to do it."

She was as good as her word, buying the land, studying plans, ordering the cabin kit. The shell, with notches cut and pieces fitted together, had already been assembled at a log yard. Once shipped to her property in Fairplay, it would take between three and four days to construct.

Once she'd built them a hideaway, she'd make sure Luke slowed down. Nothing in life meant anything if he wasn't there to share it with her.

He'd taken exquisite care of her over the years, helped her come to terms with her career and her place in the world. Now she felt it was time for her to care for him, even though she knew he would fight her every step of the way.

She asked him to take some time off and come with her, but he declined, saying he had business to take care of.

Natalie knew the night Luke had spent in the emergency room had frightened him, but he was too scared to admit that parts of his life had changed.

It terrified him, not being in control.

He was the sort of man who thought he could will his body to obey him. He took excellent care of himself. He simply pushed himself harder and farther than most men did, in every aspect of his life.

She understood him with an instinct honed from years of living with and observing him. Knowing she was up against impossible odds, Natalie decided she was going to attempt what she'd sworn never to do. She was going to try to change Luke Garner.

A tough challenge, but one she had to meet.

Monique understood, and never said anything about dropping out at the height of her career. As hot as Natalie was, even six months wouldn't make a difference.

She bought a hunter green Ford Explorer right off the showroom floor, packed enough comfortable clothing for the duration of the project and stocked up on supplies. Then she drove out to Fairplay and building began.

Otis wandered over on the second day, Tanner dogging his heels.

"Need any help?"

She sized him up in a heartbeat, liked him instantly. Otis was a godsend. He became the unofficial head of the construction crew, motivating the men and keeping morale high as the cabin shell began to rise toward the bright blue sky. Tanner became the unofficial mascot of the project.

Natalie worked right alongside the men, learning as she went. Her thoughts were feverish. She'd make Luke move his base of operations to Fairplay. What with faxes and computers, a business could be run outside the major cities. The slower pace of life would be good for him. The air was cleaner, the people friendlier.

Living closer to nature, he would heal.

She decided he'd been protecting her too much, doing too much for her. She'd contributed to the stress in his life with the confusion of her career. A career that was beginning to mean less and less to her.

Nothing mattered if he wasn't part of her life.

She wanted him to be happy. She wanted to see him relaxed and healthy. She never wanted to see him in such pain again.

Natalie made friends with the locals. She met Pete and Sam, Mae and Mike, Cora and Arnie, the owner of the J Bar J. The people, the mountains, the stars and the endless, open blue sky began to heal her raw emotions. And the small Colorado town wove a spell around her.

Mae's sister died, and Natalie spent evenings with the older woman. And it seemed to Natalie that the universe was telling her, in a very unsubtle way, that life was precious and to be appreciated.

Every second.

She called Luke on the phone every single evening, and drove to Denver on two different weekends to spend the night. He surprised her by driving to Fairplay five weeks into the project.

Natalie saw the black Porsche heading slowly up Clark Street, and she put down her hammer and approached the sleek sports car.

He'd never been to Fairplay before.

She took him on a tour, showed him all the work that had been accomplished and hoped he would find it as enchanting and relaxing as she did.

And he surprised her again, telling her he was taking the next three weeks off and helping her finish the cabin.

It worked. At first. They camped out beneath the stars, made love and woke up with the sunrise. But within two days, they were fighting.

"Stop it, Nat. I won't have you hovering around, waiting for me to have more chest pains."

"That's not what I'm doing."

"The hell it's not!"

She'd promised herself they weren't going to fight, but the argument escalated quickly.

"We've both got to slow down, Luke! None of this is worth it if we're not alive to enjoy it!"

"I'm not dying, Natalie. At least, not today—"

"Oh, you think you're so damn funny."

He caught her up in his arms, calming them both, stilling the torrent of frustrated words.

"It wasn't a heart attack," he whispered, holding her close.

"The pain, Luke, you were in such pain—"

"And I'm all right now. I'm slowing down, Natalie."

She glared at him, and he laughed.

"You're going to die, Luke."

"We all are, eventually. But I'm not planning on going any time soon."

They sat down within shouting distance of the cabin. Otis and his men were working steadily and had discreetly ignored their shouting match.

Natalie refused to look at Luke, pulling at clumps of grass instead.

"Is that what this cabin is all about?" he asked.

"Partly."

"It might have helped if you'd talked to me, instead of just running away and doing it."

"I had to do something."

"I know." He took her hand and pulled her gently toward him. "Remember when I wanted to make a few phone calls about Marta on your behalf?"

"Yeah."

"I felt pretty helpless."

It was a big admission, from Luke.

"I hated seeing you hurting so badly."

"I couldn't bear seeing you in so much pain."

"What's the plan?" he said, and she knew he meant the cabin.

"We move here, I quit modeling, you operate the business out of here and we live a simpler life."

He threw back his head and laughed, and she squelched the urge to punch him.

"We'd be at each other's throats in three weeks."

"No. Things changed for me after that night in the hospital. Nothing is as important to me as you are."

He eased her onto his lap and held her tightly.

"You're almost there, Nat. At the top of the world. And I can't afford to retire just yet. Maybe in about three more years."

"You'll be dead by then."

"Not if I can help it." He cupped her chin, turning her head so she was forced to meet his eyes. "If I go before you do, I'll make a deal with the Big Man and come back for you."

The thought made her laugh, Luke negotiating at heaven's gate.

"I haven't heard you laugh in a while."

"There hasn't been much to laugh about."

"I've already moved most of the business to Denver. We can come out here on the weekends. I promise you, Nat, I'll do nothing but relax."

She eyed him, knowing her suspicion was clearly expressed, and he laughed.

"My heart's just fine, baby. Feel it." Taking her hand, he placed it over his chest, against his blue T-shirt.

"It's beating kind of fast."

"That's because of you."

She met his eyes, then glanced away. Damn the man, he infuriated her no end, but he could still bring her to her knees with just a look.

"Are you needed around here for the rest of the day?"

"Otis can look after things."

"We could check into a hotel. I'd kind of like to rest in a bed as opposed to a sleeping bag. My delicate heart, you know."

He was impossible.

She deliberately let her hand stray toward his lap. "Don't you mean your heart-on?"

He groaned at the pun. "Your jokes are going to kill me. Let's go." He stood up, then pulled her after him.

Within half an hour, they were in bed.

THE CABIN WAS FINISHED right on schedule, and Natalie threw a housewarming to end all housewarmings. She and Luke managed to spend two weekends in Fairplay, but gradually business demands began to encroach on his time.

She had to fly to New York more often than she wanted to, but she couldn't give up her career just yet. Luke had worked too hard, done too much for her. She couldn't toss it all aside.

Yet a part of her wanted to. She began to think about staying home with Luke, creating more of a home for the two of them. Planting a garden. Making a quilt. Baking bread.

She began to think about babies.

They were everywhere, in strollers, in car seats, in people's arms. In cafés, at the movies, on television. And she found herself powerless against a hunger that began to grow inside her, a feeling that threatened to wipe out all rational thought.

She knew, on an intellectual level, that what she was experiencing was a biological drive designed to perpetuate the species. She understood that, and the fact that her body was basically a reproductive machine. She knew she was a healthy female, headed toward her thirties, and that all these feelings were perfectly normal.

She also knew, on a perfectly emotional level, that she wanted to have Luke's baby, and a part of her heart would always remain empty until she did.

Jane had married her rock star while they'd been living in Europe, and she'd given birth to her first child, a little girl. She asked Natalie and Luke to be godparents to her baby, and they flew to London for the christening.

Holding that baby in her arms, when she was so hungry for a child of her own, was one of the hardest things Natalie had ever done. But she swallowed her feelings. It was Jane's day. The celebration was for Jane, her husband, Gordon, and their beautiful baby girl, Emily.

She slept all the way home on the Concorde, her emotions brutally raw, exhausting and far too close to the surface.

Natalie kept her thoughts and feelings to herself, turning inward. Brooding. She'd known the rules of the game when she'd moved in with Luke, and it was unfair of her to suddenly demand a change. Luke had told her, point-blank, that he had no real desire for a family.

What she had to do, she told herself fiercely, was to concentrate on what she did have and be thankful for that.

It didn't work. Her heart kept battling with her head, and by the time she was in competition for the position of spokeswoman for Siren Cosmetics, she was tearing up whenever she saw a baby. Anywhere.

She'd find a bathroom, lock herself into the privacy of a stall and sob.

Monique was the only one who suspected.

"You're losing weight, my darling," she said one morning as they shared coffee in her office.

Natalie didn't reply.

"Such sad eyes," Monique murmured, reaching for her morning cigarette.

Natalie sipped her coffee, hoping Monique would change the subject.

"I couldn't have children," the older woman said quietly. "I wanted a baby with all my heart, but the doctor said it would be impossible."

"I'm sorry." Natalie set her coffee down. She'd always assumed Monique hadn't wanted children, and the woman had done nothing to make her believe otherwise.

Until today.

"Wilhelm didn't leave me, and I was always grateful to him for that. He'd wanted children, but he told me he wanted me more than any child. I still miss him terribly."

Natalie remained silent. Listening.

"I almost destroyed my marriage, wanting something that was impossible. Do you understand what I'm telling you?"

"Yes."

"I feel for you, *minou*. To be caught in such an emotional place is painful."

"I didn't want children at first. But now I can't think of anything else. I don't want them with any other man but Luke."

"I know. Tell me. Talk to me, Natalie. Don't keep it all inside. But don't torture yourself anymore. Acceptance of what you cannot change is one of life's more difficult lessons."

Monique helped her through that time and, ironically, because Natalie didn't really want a career, her own skyrocketed. The competition for the Siren position narrowed to six models, then three, then down to Natalie and a hot model from another agency.

Monique called her with the good news.

"They want you, Natalie."

The deal was the culmination of her career. Millions of dollars in exchange for the exclusive use of her image.

Monique saw through her false animation.

"You have time, darling. Who knows, Luke may change his mind. He loves you, and love has a way of working things out."

Natalie nodded, overcome by her emotions. After she hung up the phone, she lay down in the bed she shared with Luke and pulled the covers over her head.

SHE CAME DOWN with a throat infection three days later.

It refused to leave, hanging on for several weeks. Finally, one morning Luke suggested she see a doctor. Knowing how much doctors and hospitals upset her, he arranged an appointment with a friend of his, a specialist.

The usual was suggested. Stay home, sleep, plenty of rest. She filled the prescription for antibiotics on the way home, then fell into bed, emotionally and physically exhausted.

With the Siren shoot coming up, she couldn't afford to be sick. Natalie concentrated on getting better, and within a week she was up and about, her old self. Luke cautioned her to finish out her prescription to insure her good health continued.

They attended a party over the weekend and came home laughing and happy, eager for each other after their short abstinence. Their coupling was dark and swift, hungry and urgent. He loved her fiercely, letting her know how much he'd missed her.

They made love again in the morning before he left for work. Luke took a quick shower and dressed while she slept, then kissed her one last time before leaving for his office. She lay in bed, soft and warm and sated, and remembered what he'd done to her. And smiled as she slept.

Their days fell into a pattern. Natalie didn't think beyond the Siren shoot. The first series of print ads was to be shot in Greece, on an island in the Aegean. She was to be dressed as a Siren, on an island surrounded by the sea, seductive and powerful.

She rested, relaxed and enjoyed Luke's company. He'd rearranged his schedule so he could accompany her on the shoot for a few days, and she was looking forward to a stretch of uncomplicated time with the man she loved near such natural beauty.

She began to feel sick in the morning. Her breasts hurt. The smell of food made her feel nauseous. And she was terribly tired.

Natalie put the various changes down to nerves.

The Siren campaign was going to transform her life once again. Luke had teased her once about being a chameleon, and it was true. She'd gone through so many transformations during the course of her career, sometimes she felt she didn't really know who she was.

But the final transformation in store for her was certainly the most powerful and transcended anything she'd ever experienced.

She was pregnant.

Chapter Eleven

"Looks like snow," Otis said, gazing into the sky.

Luke was sitting on the back porch of the cabin with the older man, enjoying his first cup of coffee this morning. Natalie was still asleep upstairs, and he hoped she'd rest a few more hours, at least.

"How can you tell?" There was nothing in the cloudless blue sky that indicated to him the weather was going to change.

"I can smell it." Otis sighed, then finished his coffee and set the stoneware mug down on the arm of the white Adirondack chair. "Damn, you make a good cup of coffee. Wish you could teach Mae."

Luke had discovered, during the course of fixing Otis's coffee, that the man liked it black as night and thick as mud. Apparently it was the *only* thing Cookie had done correctly on the trail, and Otis remembered that strong coffee fondly.

His dog, Tanner, lay stretched out beside him, crunching softly on a dog biscuit. He'd already gone through the entire jar of treats, but Luke had discovered more in the pantry.

"I'd like you to teach me how to make those flapjacks."

Otis raised an eyebrow. "Do much cooking on your own?"

"Not a lot."

"High time you learned, with a baby on the way." Otis liked babies, and Luke could tell he was looking forward to the arrival of Natalie's.

"Well, Luke, I could make you and the little mother some for breakfast, and you could watch how I do it."

"I'd like that. More coffee?"

Otis gave him the empty mug. "This is about as close to heaven as it gets," he said, reaching down and scratching Tanner's ears.

Luke couldn't have agreed more.

He'd had a little more time to sort out his feelings concerning Natalie's pregnancy. There was only one thing he was sure of.

He was going to let her tell him in her own way.

Luke didn't want to ruin such a special moment. Again. After all, he'd already done it once by completely forgetting the dinner she'd planned.

The second thing he'd realized was that Natalie had unintentionally provided him with the most perfect of reasons for slowing down.

A cabin in Fairplay wouldn't have been enough to do the job. He would have found excuses, another deal to close, another merger he just had to have a part in.

He'd always found the world of business incredibly exciting, almost addictive.

But a child was another matter altogether.

He'd lain awake last night, listening to her slow, steady breathing, and thought about the miracle they'd created together. Totally out of their love for each other.

Luke believed he even knew the night their child had been conceived. He'd called Natalie's gynecologist in Denver earlier this morning. By acting as if he already knew about the blessed event, he'd found that the doctor estimated Natalie had been roughly eight weeks along when she came into his office.

That meant she'd been nine weeks pregnant the night of the dinner, and would be ten weeks pregnant in a few more days.

They'd conceived their child the night after one of his client's parties. Luke remembered the evening clearly, because he'd been in a state of complete sexual frustration.

He hadn't made love to her for almost a week because of her throat infection. She hadn't been feeling up to it, and he'd been aware of how wretched she'd felt.

But that night, she'd made it clear she wanted him as much as he wanted her. That night they'd made love, and the morning after, as well.

Their short, enforced abstinence, combined with her antibiotics reacting with her birth control pills, had created the perfect conditions for conception.

Luke was an expert at rolling with the punches. He changed his mind quickly and efficiently during the course of a business deal, let alone a business day. Sometimes what happened forced you to look at what you were doing in an entirely new way.

A baby was a major change. Becoming a father, preparing himself for the event in his heart and mind, was the biggest change he'd ever considered. A major life passage.

Life was funny. He wondered if they ever would have become parents if Natalie hadn't accidently become pregnant. And he doubted it. Though she'd been attempting to get off the fast track for the past few months, he'd still been enamored with it, wanting to climb higher, push himself farther.

Now he was looking forward to another sort of challenge.

And Luke wondered, as he stared out the kitchen window, at the wisdom of fate and the funny turns life took. Somehow, in retrospect, he'd found that whatever happened turned out to be exactly what had to happen.

He had no doubt he would make his mistakes as a parent. He'd try not to be as strict as his own father had been, but he'd probably make many of the same errors.

But he and Natalie had each other, and if love counted for anything, their child would be far richer than all the wealth he'd amassed over the course of his life.

"Am I gonna get that coffee sometime today?" Otis asked, a hint of laughter in his deep voice. He was standing in the doorway, Tanner behind him, his tail wagging.

Luke started. He'd set Otis's mug down on the kitchen counter, but hadn't reached for the pot of coffee. He did now, filling the mug and handing it to the older man.

"It's all right. Babies tend to addle a man's brain. Muck up his thinking process. You think this is bad, wait till that little one arrives."

Luke hadn't thought that far ahead. He'd been thinking about how Natalie would look in the months to come, her body swollen and ripe, visual physical evidence of how well they'd loved each other. He thought of the emotional support she would need to see this pregnancy through to completion. And he thought of her absolute and total fear of hospitals.

No wonder she'd run away to Fairplay. Doc had delivered scores of the town's infants at home, in their family beds. If Luke knew Natalie, she'd find a way to remain out of the hospital and give birth right upstairs.

Luke found that he liked the idea of Doc delivering their child. Just as he liked the idea of raising their son or daughter in a place like Fairplay. Oh, they'd travel all over the world. He'd take his family everywhere with him. But they would always have this cabin to come home to. Just knowing it was here would be enough.

"You're smart to let her sleep," Otis observed as he sipped his coffee. "Leaves you less time to sort out her moods."

"That's a fact." Luke poured himself another cup, then joined Otis at the kitchen table.

SHE LAY IN BED and thought about why she hadn't been able to tell him about the baby.

It wasn't that she thought Luke would be mad at her.

She wasn't even sure if he'd leave her or not.

After last night, when he'd come to bed and slipped his ring on her finger, she'd fallen asleep with a sense of total security. And this morning, waking up and staring at the ceiling as she tried to sort out her thoughts, she realized that Luke had always been there for her, no matter what.

From the time he'd first insured their meeting at the charity ball to offering his emotional support in Paris, from taking her away to Aruba to helping her fight ugly rumors so damaging to her career, he'd always been there.

He'd believed in her when she hadn't been able to believe in herself. He'd had confidence that she'd go straight to the top of her chosen profession, and with his love and support, she had.

Natalie had very few illusions left about the world. She knew, with utter certainty, that she never would have climbed as far and as fast as she had without Luke by her side.

Now she was going to ask him to stay by her side throughout another sort of endeavor, one that he'd never asked for. And never really wanted.

Yet she wasn't even sure of that any more.

She sat up in bed and reached for her robe. Maybe her hormones were making her crazy and causing her to see what she wanted to see. She'd always known Luke would make a wonderful father. But the question had always been, did he want the role in the first place?

Monique hadn't believed their relationship would last. Neither had Mick. But it had.

Four years ago, he'd bought a dance for an outrageous amount of money, claimed her as his own on the dance floor, swept her off her feet, and her world had never been the same.

Four years later, she was going to tell him he was going to become a father.

They had more than enough money to raise a child, that wasn't the issue. It was a question of desire. Though nothing truly nightmarish had ever occurred in any of the foster homes she'd been raised in, and some of them had been quite nice, Natalie had never truly felt wanted.

She'd been a lonely child, missing her father, her grandmother, but especially her mother. She'd never been neglected or abused, she'd just never felt special.

She wanted her child to feel special. Wanted. Cherished.

Loved.

The only hope she had was that the love Luke had for her would carry over to the child they'd created. His actions over the past few days, especially last night, reassured her. Before, she'd felt as if she had to tell him.

Now, she wanted to.

But she wanted it to be a special moment. She didn't want to just blurt out the news and be done with it. The dinner she'd prepared hadn't gone as she'd planned it, but there had to be a way to make what she wanted to share with him a memory they'd both treasure.

She reached into one of the drawers in the bedside table and took out a package of crackers. Two or three usually did the job. She didn't feel that bad this morning. She actually felt rather good.

Within minutes, she was in the bathroom and stepping into the shower.

LUKE HEARD THE SHOWER come on, and he and Otis got to work making breakfast.

When Natalie came downstairs, a feast awaited her.

She looked good, Luke thought, studying her covertly. Her hair was still damp, and she'd dressed in jeans and a persimmon-colored sweater. He frowned at her bare feet but knew better than to start the day with an argument.

This was a day for sweet-talking, as Otis had reminded him.

"Breakfast?" he asked.

"I can't believe the two of you!"

"Don't give Tanner any bacon," Luke said as he set a flapjack-filled plate down in front of her. "He's already had three pieces."

He watched as she ate, and could sense she was a lot less nervous. She'd tell him about her pregnancy soon, he was sure of it.

They took coffee into the living room and were sitting and relaxing by the fire Otis built when they heard the knock on the door.

Pete and his grandson, Mike, stood on the front porch, their arms piled high with brown paper bags.

"Annie sent me over with some things," Pete said, referring to his wife of almost forty-seven years. "Thought you might enjoy 'em."

Pete and Mike trooped into the kitchen and started unloading their bags. Glass canning jars in a rainbow of colors filled the counter. Sweet pickle chunks, pickled beets, dills. Pumpkin pickles, fresh vegetable relish, corn relish. Jams, jellies and preserves.

"Doc thinks it's going to be a long, cold winter," Pete announced, as if that was perfect justification for what he and Mike had brought over.

"They're beautiful," Natalie said as she held a glass jar of strawberry jam up to the light. "I can't thank her enough."

"T'weren't nothing. She always goes overboard with the canning," Pete replied, handing Natalie the jars as she arranged them in the large pantry.

Luke gave the older man a pointed look, which he just as pointedly ignored.

Luke poured coffee for Pete and a glass of apple juice for Mike. They all returned to the living room, and Pete began to tell another one of his stories.

Mike had managed to sit next to Natalie on the sofa, and Luke studied them together. She looked happier than she had in a long time. Rested. He saw the way her hand ruffled Mike's hair affectionately.

She'd be the best mother a child could ask for.

Everyone heard the car horn, and they all turned their attention to the front door. When the knock came, Natalie jumped up and answered it.

Sam stood on the front porch, his hat in his hands.

"You see, ma'am," he began nervously, "my son drove in from the city, and we chopped us enough wood to last us through the next five winters. I'd be much obliged if you'd take some of it off my hands, at no cost to yourself, of course."

Luke came up behind Natalie and glanced out the front door. Sam's yellow pickup truck was parked in the driveway, the truckbed piled high with wood.

Sam didn't give either of them a chance to reply.

"Like I said, ma'am, I'd be much obliged."

"Thank you, Sam," Natalie said, and Luke could hear the amazement in her voice. The people of Fairplay were generous, but this was going over the top.

She stayed inside with Mike and made him a few flapjacks while all the men bundled up and unloaded the wood.

"You guys are about as subtle as a cattle stampede," Luke muttered under his breath as he hoisted another log out of Sam's truck.

"We take care of our own," Otis replied.

"Thought she would've told you by now," Pete added with a grin.

"Nice engagement ring," Sam observed.

By the time the wood was unloaded and the yard cleaned up, it was close to noon. Otis called Mae at the Nugget, and she sent up some chili and corn bread, along with a pumpkin pie and some apple dumplings.

"By God, that woman sure can cook," Pete said, sitting back after having demolished a second bowl of red.

"That's a fact," Sam replied. He was at the sink, doing the dishes, having already told Natalie and Luke to sit down and take it easy.

"Going to the big dance tonight?" Otis asked.

"The dance!" Natalie said. "I forgot all about it. Oh, Luke, can we go?"

"I was going to ask you this morning," he said, feeling a bit testy. "But there never seemed to be the right *private* kind of moment."

"I can take a hint," Pete said. "These two lovebirds want some time alone, and who can blame them? We'll see you tonight." And with that, he bundled up his grandson, shrugged on his jacket, and the two of them went out the back door.

"I'll be outta here as soon as the dishes are finished," Sam said good-naturedly. Otis was drying and packing them in Mae's basket.

Within thirty minutes, they were alone together in the living room, enjoying the crackling fire. The weather was brisk, and as Luke looked out the window at tree branches bending in the wind, he remembered what Otis had said about snow.

Winter was on its way to Fairplay.

The phone rang, breaking the silence, and Luke picked up the receiver.

Peter, his personal assistant, informed him that Mr. Numata, the president of the Akira Corporation, had flown into Denver this morning and wanted to see him as soon as possible.

"I thought I could arrange dinner for the two of you," the young man said, his tone as brisk and efficient as always.

The Akira Corporation. The limited merger. If Mr. Numata had flown in all the way from his main office in Japan, that meant he was ready for the final negotiations.

He'd forgotten all about the deal over the past few days. The news that he was about to become a father had obliterated everything else from his brain.

He glanced at Natalie, curled up beneath the wool afghan on the comfortable couch. And he knew he couldn't leave her, no matter what happened with the deal.

"I can't. You'll have to explain to Numata that I have family responsibilities."

"Sir, I don't mean to question your judgment—"

Which of course was exactly what Peter was doing, but in an extremely tactful way.

"—but he *has* come a long way."

"I realize that, Peter." Natalie had fallen asleep, her head cushioned by one of the throw pillows, and as

Luke continued the conversation, he tucked the afghan around her bare feet. "If there was any way I could make it into Denver, I would. But I can't. He'll just have to understand."

"I see," Peter said.

But he clearly didn't.

Luke hung up the phone and stared out the window at Otis's Victorian house across the street.

In that short space of time, within the confines of a single call, making the deal had stopped being the world to him. Business was business and would always be exciting, but it would never again hold the central place it so effortlessly had.

If he was honest with himself, he would acknowledge the fact that Natalie had always come first. What she'd needed had always taken precedence over any deal. Now, with their child to consider, that commitment had deepened.

He'd made the right choice. There would be other deals, but he'd never have this moment with Natalie again. He'd never be able to regain this time with her.

He only hoped that she would tell him. Soon.

NATALIE HADN'T HAD this much fun anticipating a date in a long time.

She started getting ready for the dance over an hour before they had to leave. She knew she hadn't been particularly good company these last few days at the cabin, and she wanted to go out with Luke and play. Kick up her heels. Raise some hell.

And Fairplay was the right place to do it.

The locals knew how to have fun. Even back in the days when Fairplay had been a mining town and the buildings had been crude tents pitched in the mud, there had always been plenty of good times, what with gambling, numerous saloons and wild, wild women.

After dinner, she retreated upstairs to get ready.

She chose jeans and a red ribbed pullover sweater. The style was deceptively sexy, as the neckline slipped down one shoulder, then the other. She'd wear her black bustier underneath, and black lace panties. Black cowboy boots finished her outfit.

She styled her hair into a French braid and applied makeup sparingly. Having to wear so much of it when she worked, Natalie didn't like to wear it at home. But she was intent on enchanting Luke tonight, so she carefully made up her face, then applied his favorite perfume. It smelled stronger than it usually did, but she assumed it was because of her hormones acting up again.

Her efforts were rewarded by the look on his face when she walked down the stairs.

It was all in his eyes.

He didn't look bad himself, dressed in jeans, a black cowboy shirt and black boots. All he needed was a gun belt and a black hat and he could have been the gunslinger who rode into town looking for trouble.

Well, she planned on giving him a little tonight.

She made sure her body brushed against his when he helped her on with her jacket, then took his hand as they headed down the porch steps and toward the J Bar J.

It wasn't that long a walk, and she'd been feeling pretty good today. She'd slept on the couch until dinner, so she had plenty of energy.

Tonight would be magical, she promised herself.

Tonight, she would tell him.

SHE'D LOOKED like every dream he'd ever had, coming down those stairs.

If he was honest with himself, Luke thought as they walked to the J Bar J, he'd been as superficial as any male in wanting Natalie. Her looks had attracted him at first, so strongly that even if she hadn't had a brain in her head, he would have found it hard to part with her.

But she was everything he'd ever wanted in a woman.

Their attraction to each other had been strong from the start, and probably saved them from splitting up several times. Neither of their careers had been conventional, and certainly neither had been easy.

But they were together now, and that was what mattered.

The J Bar J was packed, and excitement hummed in the air as the musicians tuned up their instruments. A fiddler would be brought out later, and a country and western band would be up first.

He spotted Otis and Mae at the bar, giving some good-natured trouble to the bartender. Pete and Annie were visiting with some of their friends, and Sam and Cora were eyeing each other across the room, neither willing to make the first move.

The women had set their hair, painted their nails and put on their makeup. Earrings flashed, lipstick was brighter. The women of Fairplay were ready to play.

The men had adorned themselves with their best pairs of jeans. They'd donned cowboy shirts in bright colors, and sported distinctive belt buckles. About the only thing they refused to gussy up was their cowboy boots.

Brand-new cowboy boots gave away a tenderfoot every time.

The bar was dark, the lighting low. The walls were paneled in a dark wood, and tables and chairs had been pushed back against the walls to make room for the dancing. The musicians were off to one side, on a small, makeshift stage, while the bar was a horseshoe shape set against the far wall of the building.

"Now, don't you look pretty tonight," Pete said to Natalie as he and his wife came up. He introduced them to Annie, who seemed even skinnier than Pete. She had bright, happy eyes and reminded Luke of a little bird.

Natalie thanked her for the preserves, and Annie blushed.

"Least I could do, considerin'—"

"My God, Annie! Did we latch the gate so Seldom couldn't get out? You know what Arnie said he'd do if he found that dog goin' through his garbage!" And with that, Pete hustled his wife across the room and out the front door.

Luke's suspicions were confirmed when he glanced at Mae and she gave both of them a misty-eyed smile.

Wasn't there anything that could be kept a secret in this town? At this rate, the entire state of Colorado would know about Natalie's pregnancy before she got around to telling him.

He only hoped that Pete and Otis had told their wives to be discreet.

Not taking any chances, he took Natalie into his arms and swung her on to the dance floor as the musicians began to play.

He stayed by her side constantly, dancing with her, sitting dances out when she tired, getting her glasses of Arnie's nonalcoholic punch and watching the people of Fairplay whoop up a storm.

Then the fiddler arrived. He was a tall man with bushy red hair and a beard. His teeth gleamed whitely as he smiled and took center stage, then tucked his fiddle beneath his chin and began to play.

The crowd went wild.

He made that instrument sing, and one of the band members took hold of the mike and began to call out square dancing steps. The floor was packed, people were jammed elbow to elbow, laughing and calling out to each other. It seemed to Luke that the floorboards trembled and the walls shook with the force of their dancing.

After about an hour and a half, the fiddler took a break. Arnie had agreed to pay him with free whiskey, so the fiddler ambled over to the bar and sat down to start collecting his fee.

Mae climbed up on the makeshift stage and surveyed the crowd.

"We're going to try something a little different this year," she called out, "in order to raise a little money to help Doc open a hospital right here in Fairplay."

At the mention of Doc's name, a good-natured cheer went up.

"So we're going to have a little auction tonight!"

Luke started to laugh as Natalie looked at him, her accusation plain in her expression.

"Did you put her up to this?"

"No. I had no idea." They were pressed together tightly, people crowded all around them. But his hand found her bottom, and he slapped it playfully.

"I won't let anyone else get you. Now, get on up there, so I can buy myself a dance."

The women crowded forward, Mae getting them into some semblance of a line. The fiddler offered to play auctioneer, and Mae volunteered to go first.

"Do I hear any offers?" the fiddler called into the crowd.

His question met with total silence.

"Oh, Otis!" Mae scolded as people began to laugh. "Don't be so cheap!"

"Fifty cents!" Otis finally called out.

Mae narrowed her eyes and put her hands on her hips.

"I meant . . . fifty dollars." It was clear the amount of money had been wrenched out of Otis's pocket.

"Going, going, gone!" They hadn't had time to find an auctioneer's gavel, so the fiddler was using one of Arnie's stainless steel soupspoons. "Now, let's get these fillies auctioned off!"

When Cora stepped onstage, she looked nervous and flustered. Luke could see her squinting her eyes against the lights on stage, trying to find Sam.

"Do I hear any offers?" the fiddler called out.

Silence again.

"One hundred dollars," Luke called out, and the fiddler banged down the soupspoon, once, twice, then three times.

"*Sold,* to the man in the black cowboy shirt."

Luke scanned the crowd, then called out, "I bought her for Sam, in return for some firewood he gave us. Go get him, Cora!"

He hadn't misjudged the situation. Cora gave him a grateful glance from the stage, then jumped down and began to wend her way through the tightly packed crowd in Sam's direction. And he didn't look too upset.

Several other women were auctioned off, amid hoots of good-natured laughter and ribald comments.

Then Natalie stepped up.

"Now here's a woman who'd warm a man's heart," said the fiddler. "Who's going to open the bidding?"

"Fifty bucks," called out a raw-boned cowboy sitting at the bar.

"Sixty," Luke countered.

"Seventy-five," said another man.

"Eighty."

The bidding was fast and furious, with Luke topping anyone's bet as soon as it was made.

They cleared a hundred easily. Then two hundred. At three, several of the men dropped out. At five, only Luke and the cowboy were left.

"Five fifty," the cowboy yelled.

"Give it up, Dalton," Pete shouted over the noise of the crowd. "She's wearing his ring."

"One thousand dollars," Luke called out, almost doubling the cowboy's bid.

The crowd reacted, clapping and cheering as the fiddler's steel soupspoon came crashing down. Luke strode to the stage, picked Natalie up and slung her over his shoulder as the citizens of Fairplay burst into applause.

"THEY'LL TALK about what you did for months," she said as they walked home together. It was almost two in the morning. The sky was cloudy, the fall evening crisp and cold. Stars twinkled brightly in the night sky.

"I couldn't let him get his hands on you."

"But it was for a good cause." She laughed as she saw the look on his face, then darted out of his reach.

"How are you feeling?" he asked as he caught her hand in his.

She knew what he was asking.

"Great. You?"

He put his arm around her shoulders and kissed the top of her head as the first few flakes of snow began to fall.

"I'll be damned. Otis was right."

They were almost in front of the cabin when he took her into his arms and started dancing.

"Luke!"

"Four years ago, Nat. Remember?"

"I'll never forget."

"Are you scared of me?" he asked, remembering the first thing he'd ever said to her.

"No."

"Good." He kissed her. "You're even more exquisite."

She looked up at him, her heart in her eyes.

"You're making me nervous," she said, remembering that first dance.

"I am?"

"The way you're looking at me," she teased.

"And what way is that?" he asked, his voice low. The years could have melted away. They could have been dancing in that New York ballroom. But it was four years later, and life was as good as it got.

"Like you'd like to take off all my clothes."

He laughed, and they continued to dance, making slow circles on the snow-dusted road.

"You don't think it's excessive, paying a thousand dollars for a dance?" she teased him.

"Depends on the dance. Depends on where we end up."

He lifted her into his arms and started to carry her toward the cabin. Letting her down just long enough to open the door, he swept her up in his arms again and carried her inside, slamming the wooden door behind them.

"THEY WERE DANCING in the snow, Mae." There was a note of wonder in Otis's voice. Though he wasn't a romantic at heart, he knew a fine romance when he saw one.

"I'd say that's a good sign. Now get to bed, you nosy old fool."

"Snow's really started to come down," he remarked as he turned off the bedroom light.

LUKE MADE LOVE to Natalie with a tenderness he'd never suspected he possessed. And he found there was incredible strength in gentleness. She responded to him on an even deeper level, holding nothing back. And it was different this time, better than ever before.

She fell asleep in his arms, and he lay awake and knew he was among the luckiest of men.

SHE WOKE HIM from a deep sleep, and it took him a minute to realize where he was, what time it was. The sky was dark, and snow was coming down in earnest.

He turned toward her and time stopped.

Her eyes were red-rimmed, her expression one of defeat. Her lips were trembling with the effort it took to form the words.

"Luke," she whispered, her eyes welling with tears. "I'm bleeding."

Chapter Twelve

He couldn't protect her this time.

He could stay by her side and do what was best for her. He could get her to Doc as quickly as possible. He could offer comfort, love, support. He loved her so much he would have given her anything he had.

But he couldn't protect her from what was happening to her body. To their baby.

He was helpless, and it enraged him. Terrified him.

"Luke—"

"I'm here, baby."

"I'm scared."

"I know. I'm right here, I'm with you."

He kept her hand tightly in his as he picked up the phone receiver, then punched out Otis's number. And he thanked God that Natalie kept an address book on the bedside table next to the upstairs phone.

Otis answered on the third ring, and Luke told him what had happened.

"I'm with you, Luke. Tell me what you need."

"Come over and get the Ford keys from me. I'll need you to start the engine and turn on the heater while I get her downstairs. I'm taking her to Doc."

"I'm on my way." With that, Otis hung up.

"Natalie," he said quietly, fighting to keep his voice calm, "I'm going to get you dressed and wrap you up in some blankets, then I'm going to get you down to the couch, then out to the car."

She nodded, but as Luke swiftly pulled on his clothes and boots, he could tell she wasn't with him. Her focus was internal, on what was happening inside her.

He pulled the blankets back and lifted her into his arms, biting his lip when he saw the bright red stain against the white bedsheets.

So much blood.

He carried her into the bathroom where he helped her to clean up and prepare as best she could. Then he dressed her as quickly as possible, in sweatpants and one of his warmest sweatshirts.

Luke heard the door slam shut downstairs and knew Otis had arrived. Taking Natalie's face in his hands and giving her a swift kiss on the forehead, he ran to the top of the stairs.

"The keys are on the coffee table, the red key chain!"

"Got 'em." Otis's voice was calm as it floated toward him. "I'll start the engine and be right back."

He returned to the bathroom. Natalie was standing, slowly making her way to the door. He swept her up into his arms and deposited her on the bed, then gathered up several of the blankets that had slipped to the foot of the bed.

"Stand up for me, Nat. Just for a second."

He wrapped the blankets around her, his movements swift and sure, then lifted her into his arms again and headed toward the stairs.

She tucked her face beneath his chin, against his neck, and he felt the warmth and wetness of her tears on his bare skin.

"Don't give up, baby," he whispered, pressing his lips against her hair. "Hang on for me, okay?"

The cold night air hit him with wintry fury as he stepped outside the front door and headed toward the Explorer. He could barely see the exhaust fumes against the dark sky and whirling snow.

Otis opened the front passenger door for him. He'd already arranged the seat so she'd be leaning back. Luke settled Natalie in, tucking the blankets securely around her and fastening her seat belt. He shut the door and turned to find himself facing Mae.

"I phoned the hospital," she said quietly. "Doc's still there." She hesitated. "Buene's closer," she said, referring to the medical center there.

"Doc's at Breckenridge."

"Even Bailey," Mae said, then stopped. She switched tactics. "Luke, you know you can't make it across that pass in this weather."

The look he gave her forestalled any further argument.

"Otis, can you give me directions?"

"Hell, boy, I'm comin' with you."

It was then that Luke noticed the thermos of coffee Mae carried. She handed it to her husband, then backed away.

"I'll phone Doc and tell him to be ready." Her eyes were bright with unshed tears. "And I'll pray."

"Thanks." Luke was already circling the car, Otis opening a door and climbing into the back seat.

It was warm inside, thanks to Otis. Luke put the gears in reverse and backed down the drive.

"That way," Otis said.

Their journey began.

HE HAD OTIS hold Natalie's hand, because he needed both of his to concentrate on the road. The snow-storm hadn't let up, and the white flakes came down so thickly he could barely see what was in front of him.

Several times they veered off the road, but he carefully put the gears in reverse, backed out and kept going.

Thank God for four-wheel drive.

The strangest things came to his mind as he drove. He'd tried to talk Natalie into buying a Jeep, but she'd ignored him and bought the Explorer on her own. Right off the showroom floor.

Whenever she was mad at him, she'd always go off and do something like that. He liked to think he had some control over her, and she liked to prove him wrong.

He thought back to an argument they'd had once the cabin was finished. What had started out as a romantic dinner had escalated into a fight. He'd been standing in front of the fireplace, furious at her, and he could remember the words he'd shouted at her.

"What the hell are you trying to do, build such a strong cabin you can protect me from death?"

She'd dissolved into tears but given back as good as she got.

"Yes! Yes, damn it, because if you go, then there's nothing left!"

He didn't dare risk a glance at her, bundled up next to him. But he thought about those words, and he knew what she'd meant even then.

If you go, there's nothing left. . . .

He didn't think she was going to die, but he wasn't sure about their baby. If she lost their child, he truly didn't know if she would be able to go on.

All he knew was that he couldn't go on without her.

Everything he'd done, from the moment he'd met her, had been for Natalie. When he'd started his pursuit of her, it had been with the idea of finding her and seeing if she could fascinate and arouse him as much in the flesh.

Her photograph had knocked him for a loop.

Reality had been a miracle.

A love like the one he'd found with her came along once in a lifetime. And only if you were very, very lucky.

As he concentrated on the road, he wondered why she hadn't been able to tell him about the baby.

Four years into their relationship, and she hadn't been able to trust him with the fact that she was pregnant.

It hurt like hell. It made him see parts of their relationship with a terrible clarity. He'd had what he wanted, and had even known what she wanted, but he'd thought he was unable to give it to her.

The baby had changed everything. Once he'd realized she was pregnant, everything had fallen into place emotionally.

A love that came along once in a lifetime deserved the sanctity of marriage. The protection of a public commitment. Natalie deserved nothing but his best. So did their child.

Now, even before they reached Doc, it might be too late.

"How many miles?" he asked Otis, his voice low.

"'Bout five more. It shouldn't be too much longer."

The snow was blinding as the car inched along the road. Luke erred on the side of caution, for if they got stuck in a deep drift, there would be no way he could get Natalie into Doc's capable hands.

Just a little longer... a little longer...

The wind was so fierce, it was blowing the snow sideways. He wondered if Mae had been right, then realized he couldn't let any doubts deter him from his purpose. Natalie needed to see a good doctor, and Doc Harte was the best. She felt safe with him. She trusted the old man.

If anyone could save their baby, Doc could.

The wind was whipping up the snow from the ground. Whiteout, the locals called it. Luke narrowed his eyes, tightened his grip on the wheel and kept going.

"Luke?"

"Shh, baby. Don't talk."

"I was pregnant."

Was.

"I'm so sorry," she whispered.

"No. No, don't be sorry." He wanted to reach for her, touch her, but he had to keep all his attention on the road.

"I wanted to tell you—"

"I know."

"—but I was scared."

He took a deep breath. "I'm taking you to Doc. He's waiting for us, and I want you to try and hold on just a little longer."

"Okay."

The trust and faith he heard in that one-word reply caused his eyes to sting, and he blinked furiously, willing himself to concentrate on the road.

He followed Otis's softly spoken directions, and soon they were pulling into the parking lot of the medical center. Otis leaped out and grabbed a wheelchair, but Luke parked the car close to the door, gathered Natalie up in his arms and took her inside.

Doc was waiting for them, and he had Luke place Natalie on an examination table, then hustled him out.

All he could do was wait.

THE SNOW STOPPED about an hour after they arrived. The sky began to lighten, but Luke and Otis sat in the waiting room and stayed silent, each lost in his own thoughts.

"Mae lost a child," Otis said quietly.

"I didn't know . . . I'm sorry."

"A little girl. Stillborn. Took her years and years to recover." Otis rubbed his hand over his eyes. "Took me just as long."

Luke was silent, not sure how to reply. He had a feeling that Otis was trying to soften the blow in his own way.

"You never forget."

Luke nodded.

Otis's eyes were red-rimmed, though Luke wasn't sure whether from tiredness or emotion.

"She's stronger than you think," Otis continued. "It amused me at first, when I heard this little lady was planning on building a cabin across from me. We see a lot of tenderfeet in Fairplay, but most of 'em don't stick around."

Luke wondered where this story was going, but found he didn't mind it all that much. Otis's voice was comforting.

"First saw her, she was holding a hammer in her hand and looking up at the sky. Skinny thing. Tall, but skinny. Took me awhile before I figured out she had a backbone to her."

Luke smiled tiredly. *That she did.*

"If she loses that baby, don't go blaming her."

"Never." His voice sounded hoarse. Rusty.

"Some men go a little crazy when something like this happens. She'll need you."

"I know."

"Coffee?" Otis's hand was solid on his shoulder. "It's Mae's, but I'll bet it's still better than what they have here."

Luke smiled then, and covered Otis's weathered hand with his own.

"That'd be fine."

WHEN DOC CAME OUT, he looked tired.

Luke got up and was by his side before he took five paces into the waiting room.

"She's fine."

"The baby?"

"A stubborn little thing, just like its mother."

Tears welled in his eyes as Doc's meaning sunk in. Luke ran his hand through his hair and bowed his head, ashamed of the sudden burst of emotion.

"She let me know how she finally told you."

He nodded, still too full of emotion to speak.

"She thought you might be mad at her."

He shook his head.

"I figured as much. I suppose you want to see her." Now Doc smiled as he looked at Luke, and Luke saw something in the old man's face that made him believe all of Doc's questions had been answered satisfactorily.

He nodded his head.

"Just for a few minutes."

Luke followed Doc out of the waiting room and down the corridor.

WHEN THEY WERE ALONE together and he kissed her, the tears finally came, stinging his eyes, filling them, overflowing.

"Luke," she said softly, wonderingly, wiping them from his cheeks with her fingers.

He kissed her again.

"I wanted you to tell me."

"You knew?"

"I guessed."

"You're not angry?"

"No."

She looked so tired, and he remembered Doc's stipulated time limit.

"I thought you wouldn't want a baby."

"I want *your* baby. There's a difference."

"That's what Doc said," she whispered, surprise in her voice.

He was a wise old man, Doc Harte.

"We'll get you better," he said. "Whatever it takes."

"Doc said he wanted to keep me here for awhile."

"I'll be with you, baby."

"You're sure it's okay?" she said, and he saw the last vestiges of uncertainty in her expression.

"It's more than okay," he whispered, never taking his eyes off hers. "It's wonderful."

THEY WERE MARRIED within a week after she was re-
leased from the medical center.

Monique flew in from New York, along with Mick
and Gina. Jane, Gordon and little Emily traveled from
London, and Maurice with his entire family flew in
from Paris.

Maurice designed the wedding gown. Natalie asked
for something lacy and romantic and ethereal, and he
delivered. Flowers were flown in from Denver, Mick's
chef made the cake—a sinfully unhealthy confec-
tion—and everyone gathered inside the little church in
Fairplay to hear Luke and Natalie exchange their
vows.

She was adjusting her veil right before the cere-
mony when Doc walked in.

"Almost ready?" he asked. Doc was going to walk
her down the aisle, while Luke had asked Otis to be his
best man. Jane was the matron of honor, and Mick,
of course, was taking the photographs.

"Now I am." She picked up her bouquet and turned
to Doc.

"You are a vision."

She smiled, happier than she'd ever been.

They were alone in the small room, and Doc lowered his voice.

"You've told him?"

"Not yet."

He sighed. "Natalie."

"Doc, a wedding's a lot to get through. There's
been so much pressure on Luke, and I didn't want to
add to it."

Doc stared at her.

"I'll tell him tonight."

He smiled. "I pity the man, but somehow I think he'll survive it."

Then he walked her down the aisle.

She and Luke had decided on a candlelight service, and now, within the gentle circle of light, she promised to love, honor and cherish, and he did the same. Father McKeeby, the minister, pronounced them man and wife, and Luke didn't wait for an invitation from the older man.

"You may now," the minister said, smiling, "continue to kiss the bride."

Everyone whooped and hollered, then they went over to the Nugget, where Mae had prepared a feast to end all feasts. The floor had been cleared for dancing, and Pete's fiddler friend had been asked to come play.

Luke had invited the entire town to the reception, and the Nugget could barely hold the crowd, so it spilled over into the Fairplay Hotel.

They cut their wedding cake and fed pieces to each other. Mae carefully wrapped the top layer and put it in her giant freezer. Mick had them pose for endless pictures, and then they danced their first dance as man and wife.

Maurice's dress was a masterpiece, carefully concealing the slight swell of Natalie's stomach. Doc had kept her in the hospital until she was past her first trimester, just to be safe. Now she felt absolutely wonderful, with energy to spare.

Pete and Sam attended the wedding, all dressed up in their Sunday best. Annie and Cora wore their favorite dresses. They'd managed to get little Mike to wear a suit.

Even Tanner and Seldom were bathed and sported brand-new bows for the occasion.

And through it all, Natalie looked at her new husband and wondered how she was going to tell him that Doc had discovered she was pregnant with twins.

Though the dancing and celebrating threatened to go on far into the night, Luke suggested they slip away a little early, and Natalie was more than delighted.

She threw her bouquet, and Cora caught it. Judging by the glances she and Sam were throwing at each other, there would soon be another wedding in Fairplay.

She threw her garter, and Seldom caught it, then raced out of the Nugget, with several of the children and Pete hot on his heels.

When Otis, at Luke's suggestion, brought around the horse and buggy that was to take them to their honeymoon suite at the Hand Hotel, Natalie doubled over laughing.

The wagon had been decorated to the hilt, with beer cans and black crepe paper. Someone had hand-lettered a huge sign that said Better Wed Than Dead, and another wag had put a hastily constructed fake coffin in back, with a dummy's stuffed legs hanging out.

"Our sentiments, Luke," Sam informed him. "We thought we'd offer you a little advice on your wedding night."

Luke smiled, his arm around Natalie.

"Never go to bed angry with each other," Sam said.

"Never," Luke replied.

"Don't keep secrets from each other," Otis added.

Natalie blushed, ignoring Doc's meaningful glance.

"And," said Pete, his fingers looped around Seldom's leather collar, "marriages are made in heaven." He grinned at the crowd gathered around. "So go ahead and harp at each other."

Everyone groaned at the terrible pun, then Luke lifted Natalie onto the buckboard's seat and climbed up after her.

Otis swung into the driver's seat, took the reins, clucked to the horses and started them toward the Hand Hotel.

As LUKE CARRIED HER through the doorway of the bridal suite, he whispered, "Welcome home, Mrs. Garner."

"Luke," she said as he set her down in the middle of the bedroom, "I have something to tell you."

"It can wait." He grinned, cocky and self-assured once again. "Get that dress off."

Once they were in bed together, she forgot about everything but the way he could make her feel. She found that marriage changed things, after all—but for the better.

"I love you," she whispered as she drifted off to sleep in his arms.

"I love you, baby." Luke shifted his weight so he could hold her more closely against him.

She watched as a sleepy grin spread over his face.

"What?" she whispered.

"You. What we've been through. What *I* went through to get you." He yawned, then hugged her tightly.

She cleared her throat as unobtrusively as she could, feeling her heart pick up speed as she thought of telling him about their twins.

"Luke?"

"Hmm?"

"There's just one more little thing I have to tell you."

"Nothing you say could surprise me," he said, and she could hear the smile in his voice.

She raised herself up on one elbow so she was looking down at him. He opened his eyes, and she saw the unspoken question in his expression.

"Oh, this just might . . ."

Take 4 bestselling love stories FREE

Plus get a FREE surprise gift!

Special Limited-time Offer

Mail to Harlequin Reader Service®

3010 Walden Avenue
P.O. Box 1867
Buffalo, N.Y. 14269-1867

YES! Please send me 4 free Harlequin American Romance® novels and my free surprise gift. Then send me 4 brand-new novels every month, which I will receive months before they appear in bookstores. Bill me at the low price of $2.71 each plus 25¢ delivery and applicable sales tax, if any.*That's the complete price and—compared to the cover prices of $3.50 each—quite a bargain! I understand that accepting the books and gift places me under no obligation ever to buy any books. I can always return a shipment and cancel at any time. Even if I never buy another book from Harlequin, the 4 free books and the surprise gift are mine to keep forever.

154 BPA AJJF

Name _____ (PLEASE PRINT)

Address _____ Apt. No. _____

City _____ State _____ Zip _____

This offer is limited to one order per household and not valid to present Harlequin American Romance® subscribers. *Terms and prices are subject to change without notice. Sales tax applicable in N.Y.

UAM-93R   ©1990 Harlequin Enterprises Limited